Rise of the Blood Moon

stephanie blakemore

Published by stephanie blakemore, 2024.

This is a work of fiction. Similarities to real people, places, or events are entirely coincidental.

RISE OF THE BLOOD MOON

First edition. September 23, 2024.

ISBN: 979-8227395658

Written by stephanie blakemore.

To my family, for being my constant source of love and strength, and to my friends, who have always cheered me on every step of the way. This book is for the dreamers who never stop chasing their stars, and for anyone who believes in the power of stories.

Rise of the Blood Moon

The late afternoon sun began to dip below the horizon, casting an orange glow through the small window. Caitlin closed her book with a soft thud, but her eyes lingered outside, where the light was fading fast. The passing of time had settled into a comfortable routine, but still, there were moments when she couldn't help but feel a shadow lurking at the edges of her mind.

The quiet life she and Sarah had managed to carve out felt safe—almost too safe. Two years had passed since her twelfth birthday, and yet, some part of her remained tethered to the unease she had lived with for so long. She could still hear the whispers sometimes, or maybe it was just the memory of them.

She sighed, standing up and stretching her arms. The room felt heavy, as if the walls themselves were holding their breath. She glanced toward the kitchen where the familiar sounds of Sarah moving about should have brought comfort, but tonight, even those seemed distant.

Caitlin's thoughts drifted as she wandered toward the doorway, her fingers brushing the worn edge of the doorframe. Just as she turned to call out to Sarah, the floor creaked under her foot, the sound louder than usual in the stillness of the house.

Sarah's voice rang out from the kitchen. "You're quiet tonight, Cait."

Caitlin forced a smile as she entered the room, leaning against the doorframe. "Just thinking, I guess."

Sarah glanced over her shoulder, her hands busy chopping vegetables for dinner. "About what?"

"Everything," Caitlin shrugged, trying to play off her unease. "I guess it's just weird... feeling like things are so normal after everything."

Sarah's expression softened. "Normal is good. We've earned it."

Caitlin nodded, though a part of her couldn't shake the feeling that this peace was fragile. Too fragile.

Caitlin watched Sarah move around the kitchen, her movements quick and practiced. After everything they had been through, it was strange how easily Sarah had settled into this rhythm. Chopping vegetables, stirring pots, humming softly under her breath—it all seemed so... ordinary.

"Want to help?" Sarah asked, glancing over at Caitlin with a raised eyebrow.

Caitlin shook her head, smiling slightly. "I think you've got it covered."

"Suit yourself," Sarah said with a smirk. "But don't blame me if I make something amazing and you miss out on all the glory."

Caitlin chuckled and wandered over to the table, pulling out a chair and sitting down. It felt nice to just watch Sarah do something as simple as make dinner. For so long, their lives had been dictated by survival, by fear of what was lurking in the shadows. Now, there was space for things like this—dinner, laughter, quiet moments.

Sarah finished chopping the vegetables and slid them into the pot on the stove. "You know, you could learn a thing or two in the kitchen. Might come in handy one day."

Caitlin rolled her eyes playfully. "I'll leave the cooking to you, thanks."

Sarah shook her head, smiling. "One of these days, you're going to surprise me."

"Doubt it," Caitlin replied with a grin.

The kitchen filled with the warm aroma of simmering stew, and for a moment, it felt like this was how things were always supposed to be—just the two of them, sharing dinner after a long day, without a care in the world.

Caitlin leaned back in her chair, letting herself relax. She didn't want to think about the past, or the lingering shadows in her mind. Right now, this was enough.

Sarah stirred the pot, tasting the broth with a spoon before giving a nod of approval. "Dinner's almost ready," she said, moving around the kitchen with practiced ease.

Caitlin stood up and walked to the window, gazing out at the fading light. The fields stretched out in front of the house, and everything looked still, peaceful. She couldn't help but feel grateful for moments like this—moments where they could just be normal, where they didn't have to think about what had come before.

Sarah's voice interrupted her thoughts. "What do you think? Bread or no bread with the stew?"

Caitlin turned, a smile tugging at her lips. "Always bread. What kind of question is that?"

Sarah laughed softly, grabbing a loaf from the counter. "Good point. I'll slice it up."

As they sat down, the familiar clinking of spoons against bowls filled the quiet kitchen. After a few bites, Sarah looked up and raised an eyebrow at Caitlin.

"So, what do you think?" Sarah asked, a hint of pride in her voice. "Is it edible?"

Caitlin took another bite, exaggerating her chewing as if she were deeply evaluating the taste. She swallowed slowly and then leaned back in her chair, tapping her chin thoughtfully.

"Hmm," she said with mock seriousness. "It's... okay, I guess."

Sarah narrowed her eyes, her spoon paused mid-air. "Just okay?"

Caitlin shrugged, trying to keep a straight face. "I mean, if you like your stew tasting like... well, a mystery."

Sarah gasped in mock offence. "Mystery? I'll have you know this is a family recipe. Passed down for generations!"

Caitlin grinned. "Passed down from people who didn't want to give away all their ingredients?"

Sarah couldn't hold back her laughter. "Alright, alright. Next time, you can cook."

Caitlin snorted. "If I cook, we'll both be ordering bread and cheese for dinner."

Sarah leaned back in her chair, shaking her head with a grin. "Bread and cheese, huh? You've really set your culinary goals high."

Caitlin smirked. "Why aim low when you can aim... lower?"

Sarah burst into laughter, nearly spilling her drink. "I think I'm beginning to see why you let me handle the cooking. You'd have us living on toast."

"Hey, I can make toast," Caitlin shot back, feigning indignation. "I'm not completely hopeless."

Sarah raised an eyebrow. "You burned toast last week, remember?"

Caitlin huffed. "That was an experiment. I was testing... the limits of the toaster."

"Oh, is that what you were doing? Because I thought you were trying to summon smoke signals," Sarah teased, unable to keep a straight face.

Caitlin crossed her arms, leaning back in her chair. "It's called multitasking. Burn the toast, signal for help. Two birds, one stone."

Sarah chuckled, wiping away a tear from laughing. "Well, next time you want to experiment with cooking, give me a heads-up so I can find the fire extinguisher."

As the laughter died down, the warm glow of the kitchen settled back into a comfortable silence. Sarah leaned forward, resting her elbows on the table, her smile softening.

"You know, it's nice, just... this," Sarah said, gesturing between them. "It feels like we've finally gotten some peace. It hasn't always been like this."

Caitlin nodded, her grin fading slightly as she thought back to everything they had gone through. The quiet life they had now felt hard-earned, almost fragile. For a moment, she wondered if it could last.

"It does feel nice," Caitlin admitted, her voice quieter now. "It's just... I guess sometimes it feels too nice, you know?"

Sarah tilted her head, watching her closely. "Too nice?"

"Like... like waiting for the other shoe to drop," Caitlin explained, fidgeting with the corner of her napkin. "Everything's good, and I'm happy, but... I don't know. It feels like something's still out there. Waiting."

Sarah's expression grew serious, the playful glint in her eyes replaced with something more thoughtful. She reached out, placing a hand on Caitlin's.

"Hey," she said softly. "We've been through hell and back. If something does come up, we'll deal with it. But right now, it's okay to enjoy this. The calm."

Caitlin gave her a small smile, appreciating the comfort in Sarah's words. "Yeah, I know. I just... sometimes I feel like I can't turn off that part of my brain that's always waiting for something bad to happen."

Sarah squeezed her hand lightly. "That's normal. But we've got each other, and we're not going back to that place. Not if I have anything to say about it."

Caitlin laughed softly, her mood lifting a little. "Well, I guess if we do, at least we'll have your mysterious stew to keep us going."

Sarah smirked, her eyes twinkling again. "The stew of legends. It'll keep us alive, or maybe just too confused to know what's going on."

Sarah glanced at the clock hanging on the wall and raised her eyebrows. "Wow, it's getting late. If we sit here any longer, we'll turn into pumpkins."

Caitlin laughed, standing up from the table. "I think that's Cinderella, not us."

"Close enough," Sarah said with a smirk. "But seriously, we should probably call it a night. Unless you want me to start charging for bedtime stories, too."

Caitlin grinned as she cleared the dishes from the table. "You're really pushing this 'charging for services' thing, huh? Maybe I'll start charging for my presence."

"Good luck with that," Sarah shot back, grabbing a dish towel. "Your presence comes with a built-in chaos fee."

As they finished cleaning up, the house settled back into its familiar stillness. The warm glow of the lamps in the kitchen gave the place a cozy feel, but something about the night outside felt different—heavier somehow. Caitlin glanced out the window one last time, watching as the last of the daylight faded into darkness.

Caitlin stretched and yawned. "Alright, I'm heading to bed. Try not to come up with any more reasons to charge me for dinner."

Sarah leaned against the counter, grinning. "No promises."

As Caitlin started toward the stairs, Sarah called after her, "Need me to carry you up? You know, like the good old days?"

Caitlin turned around, giving her sister a mock glare. "The last time you carried me up the stairs, I had collapsed, and I was eleven. That doesn't count!"

Sarah smirked. "Oh, it counts. You were totally out cold, and I carried you all the way to bed like a champ."

"Yeah, well, I'm not eleven anymore," Caitlin shot back, crossing her arms. "So no more carrying. I'm not a baby."

Sarah raised an eyebrow, her smirk widening. "I don't know, you looked pretty baby-like to me. Limp noodle and all."

Caitlin groaned, shaking her head. "That's it. Goodnight, Sarah," she said firmly, heading up the stairs.

Sarah couldn't help but laugh. "Goodnight, noodle!"

Caitlin had barely drifted off when the dream began.

She was standing in a wide, open field—one she didn't recognise, though it felt strangely familiar. The sky above her was an unsettling shade of crimson, as if the sun were setting but never quite disappearing. The air was thick and heavy, making it hard to breathe, and the horizon seemed to stretch endlessly in every direction. She could hear whispers—faint, indistinct voices that slithered through the air like the wind, wrapping around her.

The field wasn't empty. Figures stood scattered across the landscape, their faces obscured by shadow. Caitlin tried to move closer, her feet dragging through the thick, unmoving grass, but no matter how far she walked, the figures stayed out of reach. The whispers grew louder, insistent now, but still unintelligible. Every step she took felt like she was sinking, the ground beneath her softening into something cold and wet, like mud.

Suddenly, the ground shifted beneath her, and she stumbled. Caitlin looked down, expecting to see grass, but instead, her feet were sinking into a pool of dark, swirling water. Panic shot through her as the cold liquid began to rise, pulling her down, inch by inch. She struggled to move, but her legs felt heavy, as though they were being anchored by something deep below the surface.

Her heart raced as the water climbed higher, reaching her knees, her waist, then her chest. She tried to scream, but her voice wouldn't come. The figures in the distance seemed to watch her, unmoving, as the water crept up to her neck. The whispers now sounded like laughter—cruel and mocking.

Just as the water was about to pull her under completely, she saw it. A shadow moving through the water, just beneath the surface. It slithered and twisted, coiling itself around her legs, tightening like a vice. Her chest constricted as terror clawed at her throat. The shadow began to rise, taking shape—long, sinuous, with dark, hollow eyes that bore into her.

The word echoed in her mind, clear as day: Return.

Then, without warning, the water surged over her head, plunging her into darkness.

Caitlin gasped awake, her heart pounding, sweat clinging to her skin. The room was dark, but the lingering weight of the dream pressed against her chest. She tried to steady her breathing, but it felt like she was still underwater, fighting to break the surface.

Before she could even call out, the door to her room burst open, and Sarah rushed in, her face etched with concern. "Cait! Are you okay?"

For a moment, Caitlin could only blink, disoriented, her mind still trapped in the nightmare. Sarah had rushed into her room many times before when she'd had nightmares, but this felt different. The air felt charged, like the nightmare hadn't fully let go.

Caitlin opened her mouth to speak, but no words came. She was still shaking.

Sarah crossed the room quickly, kneeling beside the bed. "Caitlin, what happened? You looked like you were in a fight for your life."

"It was—" Caitlin swallowed hard, her voice weak. "It was just a nightmare."

But something in the way she said it made both of them realise that this time, it wasn't *just* a nightmare.

Sarah stayed by Caitlin's side, her eyes searching Caitlin's face for answers. "That looked like one hell of a nightmare," she said, her voice a mix of concern and relief. "You were flailing around like you were fighting off a wild animal. Did a squirrel attack you in your dreams?"

Caitlin blinked, her heart still pounding, but a small smile tugged at the corner of her lips. "More like a swamp monster," she muttered, wiping the sweat from her forehead. "Pretty sure I lost that fight."

Sarah raised an eyebrow, sitting back on her heels. "A swamp monster? And here I was thinking you'd graduated to fighting dragons by now. You're slipping."

Caitlin snorted, the tension in her chest easing just a little. "Dragons are overrated. Swamp monsters are where the real action is."

"Clearly," Sarah said with a grin. "But next time, if you're going to take on a swamp monster, try not to make it sound like you're wrestling an entire forest. I almost thought the house was under attack."

Caitlin laughed, the sound weak but genuine. "Well, sorry for the false alarm. I'll work on my dream-battle tactics."

"Good," Sarah said, giving her a playful nudge. "But seriously, you okay?"

Caitlin nodded, the fear from the nightmare fading as she met Sarah's gaze. "Yeah, I'll be fine. Just need to stop getting into fights with imaginary creatures."

Sarah stood up, stretching. "Well, next time, invite me. I've been waiting to fight a swamp monster for years."

Sarah, still grinning, plopped down on the edge of Caitlin's bed, giving her a light nudge with her elbow. "You know, for someone who's been battling swamp monsters in her sleep, you still look like a half-asleep noodle."

Caitlin rolled her eyes but smiled. "I prefer 'warrior of the swamp,' thank you very much."

"Oh, definitely," Sarah teased, reaching over to ruffle Caitlin's hair. "Such a fierce warrior... with bedhead."

Caitlin swatted her hand away, laughing. "Hey! The bedhead is part of my charm."

"Sure it is," Sarah said, sitting back with a smirk. "But if you're going to keep this up, I might have to braid your hair before bed. You know, warrior braids to go with your swamp-fighting adventures."

Caitlin groaned dramatically. "That sounds like an unnecessary amount of effort. I think I'll stick with the bedhead. It's low maintenance."

"Low maintenance and highly dangerous," Sarah agreed, nodding sagely. "Perfect for confusing your enemies."

They shared a laugh, the tension in the room all but gone. Sarah gave Caitlin's hair one last playful ruffle before standing up. "Alright, warrior. You should get some rest. Don't want you falling asleep in the middle of your next swamp battle."

Caitlin smiled, feeling lighter than she had in a while. "Thanks, Sarah."

Sarah gave Caitlin one more playful nudge before standing up, stretching with a mock yawn. "Well, I'll leave you to it then. Try not to get eaten by another swamp monster tonight."

Caitlin smirked, adjusting her pillow. "I'll do my best. No promises, though."

Sarah raised an eyebrow, smirking as she headed for the door. "If you need me, just scream—preferably not loud enough to make me think you're being eaten by a tree, okay?"

Caitlin chuckled, shaking her head. "Got it. I'll keep the drama to a minimum this time."

"Much appreciated," Sarah said with a grin as she left the room.

As soon as the door clicked shut behind Sarah, the playful smile faded from Caitlin's face. A small knot of worry tightened in her chest. She couldn't shake the feeling that something was off, and it wasn't just the nightmare.

She slipped out of bed, her bare feet making soft sounds on the wooden floor. Her eyes were drawn to the window as if something outside was calling to her. With slow, deliberate steps, she wandered over and pushed the curtains aside, her heart skipping a beat as her gaze fell on the sky.

The moon hung low, large and unnervingly close, casting an eerie glow over the landscape. But it wasn't the moon she had grown used to seeing. This one was different. It wasn't pale white or the soft silver she expected.

It was red. Deep, ominous, blood-red.

Caitlin's breath caught in her throat. The crimson light bathed the fields in an unsettling glow, casting long, dark shadows that seemed to shift as she watched. The moon seemed alive, pulsating with a strange energy that made her stomach churn.

She blinked, wondering if her eyes were playing tricks on her after the nightmare. But when she looked again, it was still there. The blood moon.

Her heart raced, and she couldn't pull her gaze away. Something about it felt wrong, like the sky itself was trying to warn her.

Caitlin stood frozen by the window, her gaze locked on the ominous blood moon hanging in the sky. The eerie red glow reflected in her wide eyes, but she didn't flinch, didn't move. The world outside felt as still and heavy as the air in the room.

The door creaked open behind her, slow and deliberate. Caitlin didn't turn, her eyes still glued to the sight before her. The sound of footsteps barely registered as Sarah quietly entered the room again, her usual teasing tone gone. Instead, she moved toward Caitlin with quiet purpose, her face set in concern.

Sarah didn't say anything at first. She came up beside her sister and placed a steady hand on her shoulder, her fingers gently squeezing as if trying to ground her. Caitlin's body tensed, but she didn't pull away, her breath shallow and her pulse quickening.

For a long moment, they stood there in silence, both of them staring at the blood moon.

Finally, Caitlin tore her eyes away from the window and looked up at Sarah. Her nerves were written all over her face, her usual confidence stripped away. She wanted to say something, but the words wouldn't come. Her mouth felt dry, her thoughts tangled in fear.

Sarah's eyes met hers, a deep crease of worry forming between her brows. They didn't need to speak to know what the other was feeling. The look they shared said enough.

Caitlin swallowed hard, her voice barely a whisper. "Sarah... what's happening?"

Chapter 2: Shadows of the Moon

Caitlin sat on the edge of the bed, her head bowed low, her hands clenched tightly in her lap. Her breathing was shallow, uneven, as if the weight of the blood moon still pressed heavily on her chest. The room felt smaller now, the air thick with unspoken fears.

Sarah sat beside her, her presence a steady anchor in the storm of Caitlin's thoughts. She didn't speak right away, just placed a gentle hand on Caitlin's back, her touch warm and reassuring.

For a long moment, neither of them moved. The silence between them was heavy, but not uncomfortable. Caitlin's mind raced, her heart still pounding from the eerie sight of the moon outside. The image of that red glow, so unnatural, was seared into her mind. She couldn't shake the feeling that it meant something—something dangerous.

"I don't know what's happening," Caitlin whispered, her voice barely audible, as if speaking too loudly would make it all real.

Sarah's hand on her back stayed firm, her eyes soft with concern. "We'll figure it out," she said quietly, her voice steady. "We always do."

Caitlin shook her head, her breath catching in her throat. "But what if we can't? What if this is something we can't stop?"

Sarah turned slightly, her expression firm but gentle. "Then we'll face it together, like we always have."

Caitlin lifted her head slightly, her eyes meeting Sarah's. There was fear in them, but something else too—a small flicker of hope, even if she couldn't feel it fully yet. Sarah's calm presence was like a lifeline, pulling her back from the edge of panic.

They sat in silence for a moment longer before Caitlin spoke again, her voice trembling slightly. "Do you think... do you think the blood moon is a warning?"

Sarah's lips pressed into a thin line, but she didn't answer right away. Instead, she squeezed Caitlin's shoulder gently. "I don't know," she admitted softly. "But we'll figure it out, together."

Sarah took a breath, trying to inject some humour into the situation. "You know, if this is a warning from the blood moon, maybe it's just telling us to avoid swamp monsters for a while. I mean, how many times do we need to battle those?"

Caitlin attempted a smile, but it faltered as a tear slipped down her cheek, unbidden. She wiped it away quickly, but Sarah noticed. The humour faded from Sarah's face as concern washed over her.

"Hey," Sarah said softly, shifting closer. She wrapped her arms around Caitlin in a tight embrace, pulling her sister close. "It's okay to feel scared. I'm right here."

Caitlin leaned into Sarah, letting the warmth of her sister's embrace envelop her. The strength of Sarah's presence was grounding, and for a moment, she allowed herself to let go of the fear that had gripped her.

"I'm sorry," Caitlin murmured, her voice muffled against Sarah's shoulder. "I didn't mean to—"

"You don't have to apologize," Sarah interrupted gently. "You can feel however you need to feel. We've been through so much, and it's okay to be scared."

Caitlin took a deep breath, letting the comfort of Sarah's words sink in. "I just... I thought I was done with all this," she confessed, her voice trembling slightly.

"We both did," Sarah replied, pulling back just enough to look Caitlin in the eye. "But whatever comes our way, we'll handle it together. Always together."

Caitlin nodded, feeling a flicker of reassurance in Sarah's words. The bond they shared was stronger than any darkness lurking in the shadows.

Sarah stood up, needing to move, to break the intensity of the moment. She stretched her arms overhead and let out a soft sigh.

"So... do you need me to sleep in here with you again? You know, in case the blood moon decides to come back and make things spooky."

Caitlin cracked a small smile despite the lingering unease. "No, I think I'll survive. Pretty sure the blood moon has had its fun for the night."

"Well, just so you know," Sarah continued, raising an eyebrow, "if it comes knocking again, I'm gonna charge extra for night watch services. This whole 'defender against ominous moons' gig doesn't come cheap."

Caitlin chuckled softly, the tension in her chest easing just a bit. "Noted. But if anything weird happens again, you better be ready."

"Always ready," Sarah replied with a grin. "I'll even bring a flashlight to shine on that creepy moon, just in case."

Caitlin shook her head, smiling more genuinely now. "You're ridiculous."

"Hey, you need someone to keep things interesting," Sarah teased, stepping toward the door. "Now, try and get some sleep, warrior. I'll be right next door—moon patrol and all."

As Sarah left the room, the door clicking softly behind her, Caitlin sat in silence for a moment. The feeling of her sister's presence lingered, but so did the unsettling sight of the blood moon. Unable to resist, Caitlin got up from the bed and moved to the window, pulling the curtain aside once more.

There it was, still hanging in the sky—deep red, ominous, and unwavering. Caitlin stared at it for a long moment, her heart heavy with uncertainty. The sight of the moon left her feeling as if the world was holding its breath, waiting for something to happen.

She sighed heavily, the weight of it pressing down on her. With one final glance at the crimson sky, she pulled the curtains shut, blocking the view.

Back in bed, she pulled the covers up to her chin and stared at the ceiling. Her mind raced, filled with echoes of her nightmare and the image of the blood moon looming overhead. The quiet of the room only seemed to amplify her fears.

Caitlin closed her eyes slowly, though a part of her didn't want to. She didn't want to fall asleep—not when the nightmares felt so real, so close, as if they were waiting for her the moment her guard was down.

But her body, exhausted from the night's events, had other plans. After a long, tense silence, sleep finally overtook her, dragging her back into the unknown, where shadows and whispers lingered just beyond reach.

The house had fallen into silence, but Sarah couldn't shake the lingering worry that tugged at her. She paced lightly outside Caitlin's room, her protective instincts still on high alert. After a few moments of hesitation, she quietly opened the door and stepped inside.

Caitlin was already fast asleep, curled up under the blankets. Sarah smiled softly as she noticed the familiar sight of Caitlin's thumb in her mouth, a habit from childhood that never quite disappeared during the most vulnerable moments. Despite everything they'd been through, there was still something sweet and innocent about seeing her like this.

Sarah approached the bed, her footsteps nearly soundless on the floor. She crouched down beside her sister and whispered softly, "You'll always be my little warrior."

Leaning in, she pressed a gentle kiss to Caitlin's forehead, her lips brushing against her skin. Caitlin stirred slightly but didn't wake, her breathing deep and steady.

As Sarah stood up to leave, she glanced back one more time, watching Caitlin's peaceful face. But before she could fully exit the room, a soft voice reached her.

"Sarah?" Caitlin's voice was barely a whisper, her eyes slowly fluttering open. A little smile tugged at the corners of her mouth, sleepy but full of warmth. "Thanks... for everything. I don't know what I'd do without you."

Sarah's heart melted, and she stepped back toward the bed, her voice soft and filled with affection. "You'll never have to find out, Cait. I'm always here."

Caitlin smiled, her eyes heavy with sleep. "Promise?"

Sarah leaned down, brushing a strand of hair from Caitlin's face before pressing a gentle kiss to her forehead. "I promise, little warrior. Always."

Caitlin's eyelids drooped, and she drifted back to sleep, her breathing steady and calm.

With one last tender look, Sarah quietly slipped out of the room, closing the door softly behind her, her heart full of love for the sister she'd always protect.

The house was quiet again, the soft hum of the night settling back into place. Outside, the wind had picked up slightly, rustling the trees that lined the edge of the property. Sarah, now back in her own room, lay awake for a few moments longer, her thoughts drifting between worry and hope. She knew Caitlin was stronger than she gave herself credit for, but the unease Sarah had felt earlier still gnawed at her.

Eventually, exhaustion took over, and Sarah closed her eyes, allowing sleep to finally pull her under.

Morning came too quickly. The sunlight streamed through the windows, casting a warm glow over the room. Caitlin stirred, blinking as the soft light coaxed her awake. The events of the previous night seemed distant now, but the strange tension in her chest lingered, a quiet reminder that something had changed.

She stretched and yawned, slipping out of bed. The curtains were still drawn, blocking out the full view of the outside world, and for a brief moment, Caitlin hesitated before opening them. The memory of the blood moon flashed in her mind, but as she pulled the curtains apart, the sky was bright and clear—no sign of the ominous red glow that had haunted her the night before.

She sighed in relief, though a small voice inside her whispered that the peace wouldn't last forever.

Downstairs, Sarah was already in the kitchen, her usual morning routine in full swing. The sound of sizzling eggs filled the air, and the smell of fresh coffee drifted through the house. Caitlin smiled as she entered the room, the normalcy of the morning helping to push aside the lingering fears.

"Morning," Caitlin said, sliding into a chair at the table.

Sarah glanced over her shoulder, a small smile on her lips. "Morning, sleepyhead. You look better today."

"Yeah," Caitlin replied, though the heaviness from the night before hadn't entirely left her. "I feel better... sort of."

Sarah set a plate of eggs in front of her and sat down across the table. "Good. But if you start seeing blood moons again, let me know, and I'll get the flashlight ready."

Caitlin snorted, rolling her eyes. "You and your flashlight."

Sarah grinned. "Hey, it's all part of my blood moon patrol."

As the morning went on, Caitlin felt the tension from the previous night ease further. The sunlight streaming through the windows made the world outside seem normal again, as if the blood moon and the nightmares had been nothing more than a distant memory. Still, she couldn't quite shake the feeling that something was lurking just beneath the surface.

"Plans for today?" Sarah asked, sitting down across from Caitlin, her tone casual but her eyes sharp with her usual protective instinct.

Caitlin shrugged, poking at her eggs with her fork. "Not much. Maybe head outside, clear my head a bit."

"Good idea," Sarah replied, leaning back in her chair. "But if you run into any ominous clouds or creepy moons, give me a heads-up. I'll bring my patented flashlight defence."

Caitlin laughed softly. "I'll be sure to do that. Maybe I'll even make you a badge—'Blood Moon Patrol Leader.'"

Sarah smirked. "You know, that has a nice ring to it. Could be a whole new career path."

Caitlin shook her head, a small smile on her lips as she finished her breakfast. Despite Sarah's teasing, the unspoken concern was still there.

It was in the way her sister watched her a little too closely, and in the way Caitlin felt a subtle, constant pressure in the back of her mind.

As Caitlin finished up in the kitchen, she grabbed her jacket and stepped outside. The cool air greeted her, and for a moment, everything felt right again. The sky was blue, birds chirped in the trees, and there was no sign of the blood moon's eerie glow.

She wandered down to the edge of the field, the grass damp beneath her shoes. Her thoughts drifted as she walked, trying to shake off the remnants of fear from the night before. The quiet of the morning helped, though a nagging voice in the back of her mind reminded her that the peace might not last.

Caitlin found a spot beneath a tree and sat down, leaning back against the trunk. The warmth of the sun felt soothing on her skin, and for the first time in hours, she let herself relax.

But just as her eyes closed, a soft rustling came from the woods nearby. Caitlin's heart skipped a beat, her senses suddenly on high alert. She sat up, scanning the trees.

"Sarah?" she called out, half-expecting her sister to appear with her flashlight in hand, ready to make another joke about patrol duty.

But there was no answer. The rustling stopped, leaving an eerie silence in its place.

Caitlin stood, her eyes locked on the line of trees ahead. The rustling had stopped, but the sudden silence felt heavy, unnatural. She hesitated for a moment, unsure if she should investigate or head back to the house where Sarah would undoubtedly have something sarcastic to say about her "jumping at shadows."

But curiosity won out.

Slowly, she stepped forward, her eyes darting between the trees, trying to catch any movement. As she neared the edge of the woods, the sound returned—a soft, almost rhythmic rustling, as if something—or someone—was moving through the brush just beyond her view.

"Hello?" Caitlin called, her voice wavering slightly, though she tried to keep it steady.

No response. Just the steady rustling, growing fainter with each passing second.

Caitlin slowly backed away, her movements careful, her eyes fixed on the dark line of trees. The further she moved, the louder her pulse seemed to pound in her ears. She could feel the cold creeping up her spine, but she forced herself to remain calm.

Step by step, she retreated, resisting the urge to turn and run outright. Whatever was making that sound felt like it was watching her—waiting.

Finally, she broke. Without another thought, Caitlin spun around and hurried back to the house, her heart racing faster with every step. Her feet barely touched the ground as she sprinted toward the safety of home.

As she approached the house, Sarah appeared at the door, her eyes narrowing in concern as she saw Caitlin rushing toward her.

"Cait!" Sarah called, immediately stepping out onto the porch, her voice sharp with worry. "What's going on? What happened?"

Breathing heavily, Caitlin stopped just short of the steps, her face pale. "I heard something... near the trees. It didn't feel right."

Sarah's expression darkened as she took a step toward Caitlin, her protective instincts kicking in. "Show me."

Caitlin's breaths grew rapid and shallow, her whole body trembling violently as fear consumed her. "No, no, no!" she gasped, backing further away, her eyes wild with terror. Her hands shook uncontrollably, and it was as if her body couldn't respond to anything but the overwhelming panic.

Sarah's eyes widened with concern as she watched her sister's body shake uncontrollably. "Cait, hey—hey, look at me!" Sarah called, her voice more urgent now, but Caitlin was spiraling, her sobs ragged and deep, her chest rising and falling too fast.

"Caitlin!" Sarah moved quickly, wrapping her arms around her sister, pulling her close even as Caitlin's body continued to tremble. "Shh, I'm here, I'm right here," Sarah whispered desperately, but Caitlin was barely hearing her now.

Caitlin's whole frame shook, and she clutched at Sarah's arms, her fingers digging into her sister's skin as if she were trying to hold on to reality. "It's there, it's out there, Sarah, it's coming for me, I can feel it!" she sobbed, her words tumbling out in broken, panicked gasps.

Sarah's expression darkened at Caitlin's unfinished sentence. She didn't need her sister to say the name; the memory of "him" was enough to send chills through her. The thought of whatever power—or person—was tied to the blood moon felt too close, too real.

"We don't know that for sure," Sarah said, her voice firm but soft, trying to offer some reassurance. "But even if it is, we'll figure it out. We've been through worse, right?"

Caitlin nodded slowly, but her unease didn't fade. "What if this time it's different?" she whispered, her voice trembling with fear. "What if this time... we can't stop it?"

Sarah felt her heart clench. She had always been the one to protect Caitlin, the one to offer strength in the darkest moments. But this—this uncertainty—was something even she couldn't predict. Still, she refused to let the fear overwhelm her, for Caitlin's sake.

"Then we'll face it head-on," Sarah said, her voice resolute. "We've gotten through every storm together, and we'll get through this one too."

Caitlin's gaze lingered on her sister, searching for the confidence that Sarah always seemed to have. She wanted to believe her, to trust that Sarah could protect her from whatever the blood moon meant. But the nagging doubt remained.

"We need to find out more," Caitlin finally said, her voice barely above a whisper. "If it's connected to him... we need to know how to stop it before it's too late."

Sarah nodded, her mind already racing with thoughts of what they could do. "We will. We'll look into everything—old books, records, whatever it takes. But first, let's make sure we're safe here."

Caitlin nodded, her body still tense but finding some comfort in Sarah's determination.

"Stay close to me, okay?" Sarah added, giving Caitlin's hand another squeeze. "We'll figure this out together. And we won't let him—whoever or whatever he is—take anything more from us."

Caitlin's breath steadied slightly, and for the first time since the panic had gripped her, she felt a flicker of hope. She leaned against her sister, grateful for Sarah's unwavering strength.

The house was quiet again, the warmth of the afternoon sunlight filling the room, but the sense of foreboding still lingered, like a shadow at the edge of their world, waiting for the right moment to strike.

"We'll figure it out," Caitlin repeated softly, more to herself than to Sarah. "We have to."

As they sat there together, the weight of what lay ahead pressed down on them both. The blood moon had marked the beginning of something—they just didn't know what. But whatever it was, they would face it. Together.

Sarah's voice was calm, but the weight of her promise hung heavy between them. Caitlin looked at her sister, the fear still clouding her eyes, but there was a flicker of trust there—trust that Sarah would protect her, no matter the cost.

"I don't want to be afraid anymore," Caitlin whispered, her voice small but full of determination. "I don't want to live in fear of what might come."

Sarah gave a soft, reassuring smile, brushing a strand of hair from Caitlin's face. "We're not going to live in fear. We're going to face this together, whatever it is. And I promise, we won't let it control us."

Caitlin took a deep breath, trying to let those words sink in. She squeezed Sarah's hand, drawing strength from her sister's unwavering resolve. "What do we do now?" she asked, her voice a little steadier.

"We keep digging," Sarah said, standing up and pacing slightly as she thought. "There's more to this than just Lethanor. I need to go back through the book. There might be something we missed."

Caitlin nodded, her mind racing. "I'll help. I can look through the old journals we found last year. Maybe there's something in there about the blood moon or any other threats."

Sarah's heart swelled with pride at her sister's willingness to face the unknown head-on, despite her fear. "That's a great idea. We'll divide and conquer."

As Sarah headed back up to the attic to retrieve the book, Caitlin moved to the small bookshelf in the corner of the living room. The journals they had discovered the previous year had been written by people who had once fought against the same dark forces they were now up against. Caitlin hadn't read them thoroughly before, but now she felt a strange sense of urgency, like there was something important hidden within those pages, waiting to be uncovered.

The house fell into a focused silence as the sisters worked. The sunlight that had once made the room feel warm and safe was now starting to dim, casting long shadows across the floor. Every creak of the house made Caitlin's heart race, but she forced herself to stay calm, her fingers flipping through the journal's worn pages.

Suddenly, her eyes landed on a passage that made her stomach drop:

"The blood moon rises, heralding the return of the old power. Even in defeat, the darkness waits, hidden, biding its time until the stars align once more. The signs will be clear—the crimson sky, the whispers in the wind, the shadows that linger where none should be..."

Caitlin's hand trembled as she re-read the words. It felt like the book was speaking directly to her, confirming her worst fears. She quickly marked the page and stood up, just as Sarah returned from the attic, a heavy book in her arms.

"Did you find anything?" Sarah asked, noticing the pale look on Caitlin's face.

Caitlin nodded, handing the journal to her sister. "I think so. This passage... it talks about the blood moon, and it sounds like what we're going through now."

Sarah scanned the page, her brow furrowing. "It's like they knew this would happen again."

Caitlin wrapped her arms around herself, trying to fend off the chill creeping into her bones. "But it says the darkness is waiting. Do you think... do you think it's coming back? That we didn't really defeat it?"

Sarah's grip tightened on the book, her mind racing. "I don't know," she admitted, her voice low. "But if the blood moon is a sign, it could mean that something—or someone—wants to pick up where Lethanor left off."

Caitlin swallowed hard. "So what do we do now?"

Sarah set the journal down, her expression grim. "We prepare. We gather as much information as we can. And we make sure that no matter what happens, we're ready."

Caitlin nodded, her fear replaced with a fierce determination. She wasn't the same scared little girl she had once been. Whatever was coming, they would face it head-on, together.

As the night began to fall outside, casting deep shadows across the fields, the sisters sat down side by side, poring over the books and journals, their minds working furiously to piece together the mystery of the blood moon. The ominous feeling still lingered, but they knew one thing for certain—whatever darkness lay ahead, they would face it, armed with knowledge, courage, and each other.

Outside, the sky began to darken, and far on the horizon, the faintest hint of red began to creep back into the twilight.

Caitlin's breaths were coming in rapid, jagged bursts, her chest rising and falling too quickly for her to catch her breath. The world around her felt as though it was closing in, spinning faster and faster. She could feel her heart pounding in her chest, the terror gripping her too tightly to shake free.

Sarah took another careful step forward, her eyes never leaving Caitlin's. "Cait, look at me. Just look at me, okay?" Her voice was steady, though her heart was pounding with worry. "You're not alone. I'm right here, and I need you to breathe with me. Slowly, in through your nose... and out through your mouth. We'll do it together."

Caitlin's eyes darted around the room, wild and unfocused, but Sarah's calm voice cut through the fog of panic just enough for her to latch onto. She tried to follow her sister's instructions, but the fear still had too strong a hold on her. "I... I can't... I can't breathe..." she gasped, her voice trembling as her body continued to shake.

Sarah's heart clenched, but she kept her voice gentle. "Yes, you can. You're safe. You're with me, and nothing bad is going to happen to you. I promise." She stepped closer, holding out her hand, not forcing but offering it as an anchor for Caitlin to grab onto.

Slowly, shakily, Caitlin reached out, her trembling fingers brushing against Sarah's hand before gripping it tightly. Sarah squeezed back, offering a steadying force. "That's it, just focus on me. Breathe with me, Cait. In and out. You can do this."

Together, they breathed—slowly, deeply. In through their noses, out through their mouths. Sarah's own breathing remained calm and even, a steady rhythm that Caitlin gradually began to mimic, though her breaths were still shaky.

The tension in Caitlin's body began to ease ever so slightly, the trembling in her hands lessening as the air finally began to reach her lungs. Her panicked gasps slowed, though the tears still streamed down her cheeks. She clung to Sarah as if her sister were a lifeline, her grip tight and desperate.

"That's it," Sarah whispered softly, her hand gently stroking Caitlin's back. "You're doing great. Just keep breathing. You're safe, Cait, I've got you."

Caitlin let out a ragged sob, her body still trembling, but the panic was beginning to ebb. She leaned into Sarah, resting her head against her sister's shoulder as she struggled to regain control. "I was so scared," she whispered through her tears. "I thought... I thought it was happening again..."

"I know, I know," Sarah murmured, her voice soothing as she held Caitlin close. "But it's not. We're not going back there. We're here, and I'm going to protect you. Nothing is going to hurt you while I'm around, okay?"

Caitlin nodded against her shoulder, her breath still shaky but more controlled. The weight of Sarah's words and the solid presence of her sister began to ground her, pulling her out of the spiral of fear that had nearly consumed her.

After a few long moments, Caitlin's breathing returned to something close to normal. She pulled back slightly, wiping the tears from her cheeks with the back of her hand, though her eyes still glistened with worry. "I'm sorry," she whispered, her voice hoarse. "I didn't mean to..."

"You don't have to apologize," Sarah interrupted gently, brushing a tear from Caitlin's cheek. "You've been through so much, Cait. It's okay to be scared, but just remember—I'm right here. Always."

Caitlin sniffled, nodding as she managed a small, fragile smile. "Thank you."

Sarah gave her a reassuring squeeze. "We're going to figure this out, I promise. Whatever's coming, we'll face it together." She glanced at the stack of books on the table, her expression hardening with determination. "But first, we're going to find out exactly what we're up against."

Together, they turned back toward the table, the weight of the unknown still looming, but the bond between them stronger than ever.

Chapter 4: Answers in the Dark

Sarah's chest tightened as she watched Caitlin standing at the edge of the unknown. The oppressive silence in the air seemed to thicken, the weight of her sister's words sinking deep into her bones. She had never seen Caitlin this vulnerable—so convinced that her fate was sealed.

But Sarah refused to give in to that fear.

"No," Sarah said firmly, stepping closer, her voice steady despite the tremble in her heart. "Nothing is coming for you, Cait. We've beaten worse before, and we'll beat this too. You're not cursed. You're not alone in this."

Caitlin's hand still hovered over the knob, her fingers twitching as if she could feel the pull of whatever lay beyond the door. Her breath hitched, and for a moment, Sarah thought she was going to open the door and step into whatever darkness waited inside.

But then Caitlin's hand fell away, her shoulders sagging in defeat. She turned to face Sarah, her eyes filled with fear and exhaustion. "Then why does it feel like it's still here? Like it never really left?" Her voice was barely a whisper, and tears shimmered in her eyes.

Sarah's heart broke at the sight of her sister—this strong, brave girl who had fought so hard to survive now standing on the edge of losing hope. She stepped forward, gently placing her hands on Caitlin's shoulders, grounding her.

"Because whatever's happening now is trying to make you feel that way. It's feeding on your fear, Cait, but we won't let it win. We'll figure this out together, just like we always do."

Caitlin's bottom lip trembled as she nodded slowly, though the doubt still lingered in her eyes. "But what if it's stronger than us this time?"

Sarah tightened her grip on her sister's shoulders, looking her straight in the eyes. "It's not. We're stronger. We've always been stronger."

A tear slipped down Caitlin's cheek, but she didn't wipe it away. "I don't want to be scared anymore."

"I know," Sarah whispered, pulling Caitlin into a tight embrace. "You don't have to face this fear alone. We'll fight it together."

They stood there for a moment, wrapped in each other's arms, the weight of the world temporarily held at bay by the strength of their bond. The oppressive air in the attic seemed to lighten just a bit as they stood together, united against the unknown.

Finally, Sarah pulled back, wiping a tear from Caitlin's cheek. "Let's go back downstairs. We'll look through those books and figure out what's really going on."

Caitlin nodded, her grip on Sarah's hand tightening as they turned away from the attic door. Together, they descended the stairs, the oppressive atmosphere lifting slightly with each step they took. The darkness above still loomed, but with Sarah by her side, Caitlin felt a small flicker of hope reignite.

As they reached the bottom of the stairs, Caitlin glanced back one last time, her eyes lingering on the attic door. The sense of dread still clung to her, but with her sister's presence beside her, it felt more bearable.

"We're going to get through this," Sarah said, her voice filled with quiet determination.

Caitlin nodded, taking a deep breath. "Together."

With that, they stepped back into the light of the living room, the warmth of their bond stronger than the shadows that threatened to consume them.

Sarah felt a chill run down her spine as she listened to Caitlin. The idea that the voices were becoming clearer—that they were saying something—only heightened her concern. She studied her sister, noting the exhaustion etched into her face, the weight of fear still lingering in her eyes despite her attempts to seem okay.

"What do you think they're saying?" Sarah asked carefully, trying to keep her own voice steady.

Caitlin shook her head, her lips pressing into a thin line as she stared at the table. "I don't know. It's like... fragments of words, pieces of a sentence. But there's something dark in it, something that feels... old. Ancient, almost. And it's growing louder."

Sarah's heart raced, but she forced herself to stay calm. She couldn't let Caitlin see just how scared she was—she had to be the strong one. "We'll figure it out," Sarah said, reaching across the table to take Caitlin's hand. "You're not going through this alone."

Caitlin looked up, her eyes shimmering with unshed tears. "But what if we can't? What if whatever's happening is bigger than us?"

"We've faced worse," Sarah reminded her, her grip on Caitlin's hand firm and steady. "Lethanor couldn't break us, and this won't either."

Caitlin nodded slowly, though doubt still flickered in her gaze. "I just don't want to go through this again," she whispered, her voice fragile.

"You won't have to," Sarah promised. "Not alone."

They sat there in silence for a moment, the weight of everything hanging between them. The air was thick with tension, the shadows in the corners of the room seeming darker than usual. But Sarah knew they couldn't afford to give in to the fear. Whatever was coming, they had to face it together, and they had to be ready.

After a long moment, Sarah stood up, gathering the books and stacking them neatly on the table. "Let's clear our heads," she suggested. "We can come back to this later, once we've had some time to breathe."

Caitlin nodded, standing up as well. "Yeah, that sounds like a good idea."

They left the kitchen and headed toward the front door, the house feeling too small, too suffocating in the wake of everything that had happened. As they stepped outside, the cool air hit them, refreshing and grounding. The sky was a bright, cloudless blue, the world outside seemingly untouched by the darkness that lingered in the attic and the pages of those ancient books.

For a moment, everything felt normal again. Peaceful.

Caitlin took a deep breath, closing her eyes as she let the breeze wash over her. "Maybe we're overthinking it," she said quietly, almost to herself. "Maybe the Blood Moon was just a coincidence."

Sarah didn't answer right away. She wanted to believe that—she really did. But deep down, she knew better. The whispers, the visions, Caitlin's collapse in the attic—it all pointed to something more. Something they couldn't ignore.

"We'll figure it out," Sarah said again, her voice gentle but firm. "One step at a time."

Caitlin opened her eyes and gave a small nod, though the unease in her expression didn't fully fade. She was trying to be strong, but Sarah could see the cracks forming, the fear that lurked just beneath the surface.

Together, they walked through the fields surrounding the house, the sound of their footsteps soft against the earth. The silence between them was comfortable for now, but both knew it was only a matter of time before the shadows returned.

Whatever was coming, they would face it—together.

Sarah's chest tightened as the truth sank in. The curse had claimed every child in their family for generations—each one unable to survive past the age of twelve. But Caitlin had survived, defied the odds. Now, with the Blood Moon rising again, it seemed Nyxora's influence had only been waiting, lurking in the shadows.

Sarah stared at the journal in disbelief, her hands trembling. "Why didn't we know?" she whispered to herself, the words barely audible in the thick silence of the room. "Why didn't anyone tell us about this?"

The bloodline, the curse, the twisted influence of Nyxora—it was all connected. Sarah had always known their family had secrets, but this was worse than anything she had imagined.

Her mind raced as she thought of Caitlin, sleeping peacefully upstairs, unaware of the full extent of the danger they were in. If Nyxora's power peaked with the Blood Moon, then Caitlin's survival, her very life, was hanging by a thread. And Sarah wasn't sure how long they had until the curse fully awakened.

With a shaky breath, Sarah closed the journal and stood, her heart pounding in her chest. She had to protect Caitlin—there had to be a way to stop this, to break the cycle before it consumed them both. But she needed more answers, more time—time they didn't have.

She grabbed the journal and hurried back upstairs, her footsteps quick and quiet. Bursting into Caitlin's room, she found her sister still fast asleep, the soft rise and fall of her chest the only sound in the room. Sarah stood there for a moment, watching her, the weight of the knowledge she now carried pressing heavily on her shoulders.

She needed a plan. Something to protect Caitlin from what was coming. But how do you fight something as ancient as Nyxora, something that had claimed so many lives before?

She placed the journal on the nightstand next to Caitlin and knelt by the side of the bed, her fingers brushing lightly over her sister's arm. Caitlin stirred slightly but didn't wake.

Sarah's voice was barely a whisper as she spoke, her words meant more for herself than for Caitlin. "I won't let this happen to you. Not now, not ever."

As she stood up, the journal caught her eye again, the words on the page etched in her mind. *The mark may vanish, but the curse does not fade—it lies dormant, waiting for the right moment to fully awaken.*

Sarah knew now that the absence of Caitlin's mark wasn't a sign of safety. It was a warning. The curse had gone deeper, hiding itself away, waiting for the Blood Moon to unleash its full power. And now that the time had come, Sarah had to be ready.

With renewed determination, Sarah left the room, her mind racing with plans. She would find a way to break the curse, to sever Nyxora's hold on their family once and for all. Because if she didn't, Caitlin would be the next victim—just another in a long line of children claimed by the Blood Moon.

And that was something Sarah would never allow.

She just had to figure out how.

Sarah's heart raced as the pieces began to fall into place. The stories, the Blood Moon, Nyxora's influence—it was all connected. The sanctuary of the Forgotten, the place her mother had mentioned, might be real after all, and it could be the key to understanding the curse, maybe even breaking it once and for all. But it wasn't just about finding the sanctuary. It was about being ready—being at the right place, at the right time, with the right purpose.

Her mind raced through the possibilities. If they could get to the mountains before the Blood Moon reached its peak, there might be a chance to find the sanctuary, to uncover the truth about Nyxora's curse and how to sever it for good. But the clock was ticking, and there was no guarantee they'd be able to reach it in time—or that the sanctuary would even reveal itself.

She needed Caitlin. They had always faced these challenges together, and this was no different. Her sister was the key to the curse, and that meant she had to come too. But how could she explain this to Caitlin, who had just been through so much, without scaring her further?

Taking a deep breath, Sarah stood up from the table and headed back toward Caitlin's room. She opened the door quietly, stepping inside. Caitlin was still asleep, the picture frame now safely back on the nightstand. She looked peaceful, the strain from the day's events softened by sleep.

But Sarah knew the peace wouldn't last. The Blood Moon was rising, and they had to move.

"Caitlin," she whispered softly, sitting on the edge of the bed and gently shaking her sister's shoulder. "Cait, wake up."

Caitlin stirred, blinking slowly as her eyes opened. She rubbed her eyes groggily, sitting up as she looked at Sarah with confusion. "What is it?" she asked, her voice still heavy with sleep.

"We need to talk," Sarah said, her tone gentle but urgent. "I found something... something important. About the curse, and about how we can stop it."

Caitlin's eyes widened slightly at the mention of the curse, but she remained quiet, listening as Sarah continued.

"There's a place," Sarah said, choosing her words carefully. "A sanctuary. It's hidden, but it might hold the answers we need to break the curse. And I think the Blood Moon is the key to finding it. We don't have much time."

Caitlin frowned, her brows furrowing in confusion. "A sanctuary? What are you talking about?"

Sarah took a deep breath, knowing how crazy it all sounded. "It's something Mom used to talk about. A place that can help people who are cursed, like us. I didn't take it seriously back then, but after everything I've read... I think it's real. And I think the Blood Moon is tied to it. We need to get to the mountains before the moon reaches its peak. That's where the sanctuary might be."

Caitlin stared at Sarah for a long moment, her face a mixture of skepticism and fear. "And you think this... sanctuary can help us?"

"I don't know for sure," Sarah admitted. "But it's our best shot. If we don't go, the curse could get worse. The Blood Moon is making it stronger, and we need answers before it's too late."

Caitlin looked down, her hands twisting in her lap. She was quiet for a long time, and Sarah could see the fear and doubt swirling in her sister's eyes. But after a moment, Caitlin looked up, determination settling in her gaze. "Okay," she said softly. "I'll go with you."

Sarah exhaled, relief flooding her chest. "Thank you," she whispered. "We'll face this together, like always."

Caitlin nodded, her expression still uncertain but resolute. "When do we leave?"

"As soon as possible," Sarah replied, standing up. "We need to pack and get moving before the Blood Moon reaches its peak. I don't know how long we have, but we can't afford to wait."

Together, they moved quickly, gathering their things in silence. The tension in the air was palpable, but Sarah was grateful for Caitlin's trust, even as the fear lingered in her sister's eyes. As they packed, Sarah's mind raced with plans—how they would reach the mountains, what they might find when they got there, and how they would face whatever awaited them.

But one thing was certain: they had to act fast. The Blood Moon was rising, and Nyxora's power was awakening. If they didn't find the sanctuary in time, the curse would consume them both.

And Sarah couldn't let that happen.

"We'll be okay, Cait," Sarah said softly as they finished packing, her voice steady despite the fear gnawing at her insides. "We've faced worse before, and we'll face this together."

Caitlin nodded, her jaw clenched as she shouldered her bag. "Let's go."

With one last glance at their home, they stepped out into the night, the crimson glow of the rising Blood Moon casting eerie shadows across the landscape. The air was thick with anticipation, the weight of the unknown pressing down on them as they headed toward the mountains.

As they walked, the whispers in the wind seemed to grow louder, almost as if Nyxora herself was watching, waiting for the right moment to strike.

But Sarah kept her focus on Caitlin, on their bond, and on the hope that somewhere, in the shadows of the mountains, the sanctuary of the Forgotten would find them before it was too late.

Sarah's hands trembled as she flipped through the journal, her eyes skimming over the cryptic passages with a growing sense of desperation.

Every word seemed to blur together, offering hints of Nyxora's power but no clear answers. The air in the room felt thick, as though the very house was holding its breath, waiting for something terrible to happen.

She tried to push the panic down, focusing on the task at hand. Caitlin needed her—needed answers, and quickly. The cryptic words Caitlin had spoken about someone dying echoed in Sarah's mind, sending a fresh wave of dread through her.

Then, a passage caught her eye, buried deep within the text:

"Those marked by Nyxora may experience visions, their souls briefly tethered to the realm of shadows. They may speak in riddles or truths, the voices of the ancient gods flowing through them. Pain often accompanies these moments, as the soul struggles to remain in the mortal realm. The curse feeds on this suffering, growing stronger with each passing moment."

Sarah's heart raced as she read the words, her mind spinning. Caitlin's cryptic statements, her pain—it was all part of the curse trying to pull her into the shadows. Nyxora wasn't just coming for her sister's body; she was coming for Caitlin's soul.

The realization hit Sarah like a punch to the gut. The curse wasn't just about physical suffering; it was about spiritual dominance. Nyxora's grip was tightening, and Caitlin was slipping away, little by little.

Sarah clenched her fists, her mind racing with a thousand thoughts. There had to be a way to sever the connection, to break the curse before it could consume Caitlin entirely. The Blood Moon was the key, but how could they use it?

Her eyes darted across the pages, searching for anything that could help. Finally, she found it—a passage about severing Nyxora's hold:

"To sever Nyxora's influence, one must face her at the height of her power—when the Blood Moon rises. The cursed must stand at the crossroads of life and death, in a place where the veil between worlds is thinnest. Only there can the bond be broken, but it requires a sacrifice—a willing exchange of life force to release the soul from Nyxora's grip."

Sarah's breath caught in her throat. A sacrifice. Of course, there was always a price. But whose life would be given? Could it be her own, or would it have to be Caitlin's?

She closed the journal, her mind made up. No matter what the cost, she would not let Nyxora take Caitlin.

Sarah rushed back to the sofa where Caitlin lay, still breathing shallowly, her face pale and her brow slick with sweat. Sarah knelt beside her, gripping her sister's hand tightly. "Cait," she whispered, her voice steady despite the fear gnawing at her insides. "I think I know how we can stop this. But it's going to take both of us, and we don't have much time."

Caitlin's eyes fluttered open, still glassy and unfocused, but there was a flicker of recognition in them. "What... what do we have to do?" she asked weakly, her voice barely a whisper.

Sarah squeezed her hand, her own heart pounding. "We have to go to the mountains—the place Mom used to talk about. The sanctuary of the Forgotten. That's where the veil between worlds is thinnest. If we get there by the time the Blood Moon rises, we might be able to break the curse."

Caitlin's brow furrowed, her face a mixture of fear and confusion. "But... how do we stop it?"

Sarah hesitated for a moment, then took a deep breath. "There's a price. We might have to make a sacrifice—something powerful enough to break Nyxora's hold."

Caitlin's eyes widened, and Sarah could see the fear rising in her sister's expression. But then, slowly, Caitlin nodded, her resolve growing stronger. "We'll do whatever it takes."

Sarah nodded, her determination matching Caitlin's. "We'll get through this, I promise."

They didn't have much time. The Blood Moon was rising, and Nyxora's grip was tightening with every passing second. Together, they would face the curse, face the ancient power that had haunted their family for generations.

And no matter what it took, Sarah would not let Caitlin fall. They would end this—together.

Caitlin's eyes, now an inky black, were fixed on Sarah, but there was no recognition—just a hollow, empty gaze. It was as if her sister was gone, replaced by something dark and ancient, something that had been lurking in the shadows all along.

"Caitlin?" Sarah whispered again, her voice barely audible, as though speaking any louder would make the terrifying reality more solid. Her fingers trembled as she gently shook Caitlin's shoulders, trying to break through whatever dark force had taken over. "Please, Cait... come back to me."

But the black voids staring back at her didn't flicker with recognition. Instead, a low, guttural voice emerged from Caitlin's lips—one that was not her own. "She is mine."

Sarah's heart dropped into her stomach, the chill of the words freezing her blood. "Nyxora," she breathed, her worst fears realized. The Harbinger had taken Caitlin.

Nyxora's voice, deep and otherworldly, chuckled softly. "Foolish girl... you think you can defy the will of the gods? She was always mine. From the moment she was born, her soul was marked. You cannot save her now."

Sarah's mind raced. Caitlin was still in there—she had to be. "Let her go!" she demanded, her voice shaking with anger and fear. "She doesn't belong to you!"

The figure that had been Caitlin tilted its head slightly, a twisted smile creeping over its face. "Oh, but she does. She is bound to me, just like all the others before her. You cannot stop what has already begun."

Tears stung Sarah's eyes, but she refused to give up. She gripped Caitlin's shoulders tighter, shaking her as if she could force her sister back to the surface. "Caitlin, I know you're still in there! I'm not giving up on you!"

For a moment, the black eyes flickered, as though something deep inside Caitlin was trying to break free. Her body shuddered violently, and for a brief, fleeting second, Sarah thought she saw the soft blue of Caitlin's eyes return. But then the darkness surged again, overwhelming whatever had been fighting for control.

Nyxora's voice returned, colder this time. "Enough. She is mine now."

Sarah's heart pounded in her chest. She couldn't lose Caitlin—not like this. Her mind raced through everything she had read, every scrap of knowledge she had gathered about Nyxora. There had to be a way to break this, to sever Nyxora's grip before it was too late.

Suddenly, the memory of the passage about the deep forest came rushing back to her:

"The curse draws them closer, where the veil between worlds is thinnest. Beware the ancient trees that hold the whispers of the old gods."

The forest. It had to be the forest. That was where Nyxora's power was strongest, but it was also where the curse could be broken—where the veil between worlds was thin enough to face Nyxora directly.

Without another thought, Sarah made her decision. She wasn't going to sit here and let Nyxora take her sister.

With a surge of determination, Sarah grabbed Caitlin by the shoulders and pulled her up into a sitting position. "You're coming with me," she whispered fiercely. "I'm not losing you."

Caitlin's body was limp, but Sarah didn't care. She would carry her if she had to.

She quickly threw a blanket over Caitlin, bundling her up to keep her warm. With one final glance at the journal, she grabbed the bag she had packed earlier, slinging it over her shoulder. Then, with Caitlin in her arms, she headed for the door.

Outside, the night was eerily still. The wind rustled the leaves in the distance, and the moonlight cast long shadows across the ground. But Sarah barely noticed any of it. All she could focus on was the deep woods that lay beyond their home—the place where Nyxora's power was waiting.

Her heart pounded in her chest as she stepped outside, the weight of Caitlin's body heavy in her arms. "Hold on, Cait," she whispered, her voice cracking with emotion. "I'm going to save you. I promise."

The deep woods loomed ahead, dark and ominous, but Sarah didn't hesitate. With Caitlin cradled against her chest, she started toward the forest, determined to face Nyxora and break the curse once and for all.

Sarah's heart pounded as she watched Caitlin struggle to breathe, the pale color of her sister's face sending waves of dread through her. Every convulsion, every retch seemed to steal more of Caitlin's strength, and Sarah knew time was running out. The urgency in her heart burned like a fire as she struggled to think, to come up with a way to stop whatever was happening.

This couldn't go on. Caitlin was fading, and the realization that she might lose her little sister, the one she'd protected her whole life, clawed at Sarah's chest like a living thing. She had to act—now.

"Cait," Sarah whispered, kneeling beside her, her voice shaking. "I'm going to get help. I'm going to fix this, okay? Just hang on a little longer. I swear I won't let you go."

Caitlin's eyes fluttered open for a brief second, glazed over with exhaustion and pain. She tried to speak, but only a small, raspy gasp escaped her lips. Her trembling hand reached out, weakly gripping Sarah's sleeve. Sarah grasped it tightly, holding on as if that alone could tether Caitlin to life.

"I'll be back," Sarah promised, her voice firm despite the tears that threatened to spill over. She squeezed Caitlin's hand, then gently set it down, brushing her fingers through her sister's hair one last time. "I love you, Cait."

With a final look at her sister's fragile form, Sarah shot to her feet and raced toward the kitchen, her mind whirling with the decision she knew she had to make. The deep forest. It was where Nyxora's power was strongest, where the curse had begun. It was the only place where she might find answers—and maybe a way to break this hold over Caitlin.

Without hesitation, Sarah grabbed the bag she had packed earlier, slung it over her shoulder, and headed for the door. Her breath came fast and sharp, fear and determination driving her forward. She couldn't wait any longer.

The deep forest loomed ahead as Sarah hurried down the familiar path toward the trees. The wind rustled through the branches, creating an eerie sound that echoed in the darkness. The forest felt alive with something ancient and foreboding, and every step Sarah took made the weight in her chest grow heavier.

As she reached the edge of the forest, Sarah paused, catching her breath. The shadows stretched long in the moonlight, and she could feel the pull—the strange, unsettling call that Caitlin must have heard before. It wasn't just the forest she was walking into. It was something far older, something tied to the curse that had haunted their family for generations.

But Sarah couldn't turn back now. Caitlin's life was on the line.

Taking a deep breath, Sarah stepped into the forest, the thick canopy of trees closing in around her like a shroud. The deeper she went, the more oppressive the atmosphere became, as if the very air was charged with Nyxora's presence.

Suddenly, a sharp whisper broke the silence. "She belongs to me..."

Sarah froze, her heart skipping a beat as the voice echoed through the trees. It was the same voice that had spoken through Caitlin—the voice of Nyxora.

"Where are you?" Sarah demanded, her voice trembling as she looked around, trying to pinpoint the source of the voice. "What do you want with Caitlin?"

The whisper came again, softer this time, almost teasing. "She is the key... the vessel. You cannot save her."

Sarah clenched her fists, fury rising in her chest. "I won't let you have her!" she shouted into the darkness. "I'll do whatever it takes to break this curse!"

The forest fell silent for a moment, the wind dying down as if the trees themselves were holding their breath. Then, from somewhere deeper in the woods, a faint light began to glow—a sickly, pale light, pulsing rhythmically like the beat of a heart.

Sarah's pulse quickened as she followed the light, her steps quickening with determination. She pushed through the thick underbrush, her hands trembling as she moved closer to the source of the glow. Whatever was waiting for her there, she knew it held the key to saving Caitlin.

As she broke through a dense wall of trees, Sarah found herself in a small clearing. In the center of the clearing stood a massive, ancient tree—its gnarled branches twisting up toward the sky like skeletal fingers. The pale light pulsed from within the hollow of the tree, casting long shadows across the ground.

And there, standing before the tree, was a figure—a woman, cloaked in darkness, her eyes glowing with the same eerie light that radiated from the tree. Her presence was unmistakable.

"Nyxora," Sarah whispered, her voice filled with both fear and defiance.

The woman turned slowly, her dark eyes locking onto Sarah with an intensity that sent a shiver down her spine. "You've come to stop me?" Nyxora's voice was a haunting echo, filled with dark amusement. "Foolish girl. You cannot break the bond that has been forged."

"I'll do whatever it takes," Sarah said, her voice steady despite the fear that clawed at her insides. "I'm not letting you take Caitlin."

Nyxora's smile twisted into something cruel, her eyes narrowing. "You don't understand. This curse is older than you. Older than your bloodline. It cannot be undone."

Sarah stepped forward, her hands shaking but her resolve unwavering. "Maybe not," she said, her voice quiet but filled with determination. "But I won't let it take her without a fight."

Nyxora's eyes flickered with something unreadable—curiosity, perhaps, or maybe even a flicker of admiration for Sarah's tenacity. But whatever it was, it was short-lived. Nyxora raised her hand, and the ground beneath Sarah's feet began to tremble.

"You will not stop what has been set in motion," Nyxora hissed. "Caitlin's fate is sealed."

As the ground quaked beneath her, Sarah's mind raced. There had to be a way—a way to break Nyxora's hold, to save Caitlin before it was too late.

And then, through the darkness, Sarah remembered the stories. The legends. "The bond can only be broken by the strength of those who are bound together."

Their bond. Hers and Caitlin's. That was the key.

Sarah took a deep breath, her eyes locking onto Nyxora's. "You're wrong," she said, her voice steady. "Our bond is stronger than your curse."

With that, Sarah closed her eyes, focusing on the connection she had with Caitlin—the unbreakable bond they had shared since childhood. She reached out with her heart, calling to her sister, feeling the pull of their love, their shared strength.

"Caitlin," Sarah whispered, her voice soft but filled with hope. "Come back to me."

For a moment, there was nothing—just the cold wind and the oppressive presence of Nyxora.

But then, in the stillness, Sarah felt it. A flicker of warmth, a tiny spark of life. It was Caitlin—she was still there, somewhere deep inside, fighting to break free.

Nyxora's eyes widened in shock as Sarah's connection to Caitlin grew stronger, the bond between them pushing back against the curse. The light within the ancient tree began to flicker, its strength waning as Sarah poured everything she had into calling Caitlin back.

"You can't have her!" Sarah cried, her voice ringing out through the clearing.

With one final surge of will, Sarah felt the bond snap back into place. The ground beneath her stilled, and the pale light from the tree dimmed to nothing.

Nyxora let out a furious scream, her form beginning to waver as the power she had over Caitlin was broken. "This is not over," she hissed, her voice filled with venom. "I will return. The Blood Moon will rise again."

And with that, Nyxora vanished, leaving the clearing in silence.

Sarah collapsed to her knees, her breath coming in ragged gasps as the weight of what had just happened settled over her. She had done it. She had broken Nyxora's hold.

But as she looked up at the ancient tree, she knew it wasn't over. The curse was still there, lurking in the shadows. Nyxora would return, and the Blood Moon would rise again.

But for now, Caitlin was safe.

And that was all that mattered.

Sarah's pulse quickened as she stared at Caitlin's wounds, her mind racing in a storm of panic and helplessness. The blood was pouring faster now, soaking through Caitlin's clothes, pooling on the floor. It was as if the very life was being drained from her sister, drop by agonizing drop.

"No, no, no," Sarah muttered under her breath, her hands trembling as she pressed cloths against the wounds, desperate to stop the bleeding. But it was no use. The blood kept coming, and Caitlin's body grew colder in her arms.

Tears welled in Sarah's eyes as she whispered, "Please, Cait... don't leave me. Stay with me, just a little longer."

Her mind raced back to the books, the journals, the cryptic symbols and fragments of information about Nyxora. The curse wasn't just attacking Caitlin's body—it was consuming her, from the inside out. And if Sarah didn't find a way to stop it, Caitlin wouldn't survive the night.

In a flash of desperation, Sarah remembered the passage about the altar in the deep forest—the place where Nyxora's power was strongest. That had to be it. That's where she would find the source of the curse, where she could confront Nyxora once and for all.

"I can't let this happen," Sarah whispered to herself, her voice shaking as she stood up, her decision solidifying in her mind.

She bent down to Caitlin, brushing her sister's pale cheek gently. "I'm going to fix this," she promised, her voice steady despite the fear gripping her heart. "I'll stop Nyxora. I'll save you, Cait."

With that, Sarah grabbed the bag she had packed earlier, her mind filled with only one thought: the altar in the forest. If that was where Nyxora's power was strongest, then that was where Sarah needed to be. She had to destroy whatever was fueling the curse before it was too late.

Sarah bent down to kiss Caitlin's forehead, whispering, "I'll be back soon. Just hold on."

Her legs trembled as she rushed out the door, the weight of the situation pressing down on her. The wind howled through the trees as Sarah made her way toward the forest, the ancient woods looming ahead like a dark, waiting presence. The pale light of the Blood Moon glowed ominously overhead, casting long shadows across the path as Sarah moved deeper into the forest.

The further she went, the thicker the air became. It was as if the very forest itself was alive, watching her, feeding off the growing tension. Every branch, every shadow seemed to whisper Nyxora's name, taunting Sarah as she pushed forward.

Her heart pounded in her chest, fear and adrenaline coursing through her veins as she approached the clearing described in the journal. There, in the center of the clearing, stood the massive tree she had seen earlier, its gnarled branches twisting into the sky like claws. And in its hollow center, the pale, sickly glow of Nyxora's altar flickered, casting eerie light across the forest floor.

Sarah took a deep breath, her hand tightening around the knife she had brought with her. This was it. The source of Nyxora's power. The thing that was killing Caitlin.

With shaking hands, she stepped forward, her eyes locked onto the altar. The ground beneath her feet seemed to tremble as she approached, as if the very earth was warning her to turn back. But Sarah couldn't stop. She had to save Caitlin.

As she reached the altar, a voice—dark, cold, and unmistakable—filled the air.

"You think you can stop me?" Nyxora's voice whispered from the shadows, her tone dripping with cruel amusement. "You are nothing. A mortal girl trying to defy a god. Your sister belongs to me. She always has."

Sarah's heart raced, but she forced herself to stand tall, her voice steady despite the terror creeping up her spine. "You won't take her," she spat, her hand trembling around the knife. "I'll end this. Right now."

Nyxora's laughter echoed through the forest, sending chills down Sarah's spine. "You are a fool," the voice hissed. "You cannot sever the bond that has already been forged. Caitlin's soul is mine."

Without another word, Sarah raised the knife and plunged it into the glowing heart of the altar.

A scream—loud, piercing, and inhuman—ripped through the air as the altar cracked and crumbled beneath Sarah's hand. The pale light sputtered and died, plunging the clearing into darkness. The ground trembled violently, the trees swaying as if in agony, and for a moment, Sarah thought the entire forest might collapse in on itself.

But then, just as suddenly as it had begun, the trembling stopped. The forest fell silent.

Sarah stood there, breathless, her heart pounding in her chest. She looked down at the shattered remains of the altar, her mind spinning with disbelief.

Had she done it? Had she stopped Nyxora?

Without waiting for an answer, Sarah turned and ran back toward the house, her legs burning as she raced through the forest, the weight of what she had just done pressing heavily on her shoulders.

By the time she reached the house, she was breathless, her body shaking with exhaustion. She burst through the door, her eyes scanning the room for Caitlin.

There, on the sofa, Caitlin lay still, her chest rising and falling in slow, steady breaths. The bleeding had stopped. The bruises and claw marks on her stomach had begun to fade, the color slowly returning to her pale skin.

Sarah fell to her knees beside her sister, tears streaming down her face as she cradled Caitlin's hand in her own. "You're safe," she whispered, her voice trembling with relief. "You're going to be okay."

Caitlin's eyes fluttered open, her gaze locking onto Sarah's. For the first time in days, there was clarity in her eyes—no pain, no fear. Just peace.

"Sarah?" Caitlin whispered, her voice weak but steady. "What happened?"

Sarah smiled through her tears, brushing Caitlin's hair away from her face. "You're safe now, Cait," she said softly. "Nyxora is gone."

And for the first time in what felt like forever, Sarah believed it.

Sarah's heart pounded, her mind spinning as she tried to make sense of Nyxora's words. The curse—the bloodline—it had always been there, but now Nyxora was speaking of it as if it were an agreement. A deal. Her ancestors? What had they done?

"What deal?" Sarah asked, her voice barely a whisper, her throat tightening with fear. She wanted to demand answers, to scream and rage, but all she could manage was the quiet, trembling question.

Nyxora tilted her head, her lips curling into that same twisted smile. "Ah, curious now, aren't we?" she purred, her dark eyes gleaming with malice. "The deal made generations ago—when your family first tried to escape the curse. They thought they could break free, but they were fools. Instead, they sealed their fate, and the fate of every generation to follow."

Sarah's stomach dropped. "What... what are you talking about?"

Nyxora stepped closer, her presence suffocating, as if the very air in the room was shrinking around them. "Your ancestors bargained with powers they didn't understand. They sought protection, freedom from the curse that had claimed so many of them. But the price? Oh, the price was high. Blood. Souls. They thought they could hide, that each generation could escape me. But that only delayed the inevitable."

Sarah's hands tightened around Caitlin, her mind racing. Her grandmother had warned her about the curse, about the darkness in their bloodline. But no one had ever mentioned a deal. A pact.

Nyxora smiled, as if reading Sarah's thoughts. "You think this started with your sister? No, no... Caitlin is merely the final piece. A vessel. The curse has been simmering for centuries, waiting for the Blood Moon to rise, for the bond to be completed. Your ancestors didn't break the curse—they ensured its fulfillment."

Sarah's blood ran cold. "You're lying," she hissed, though deep down, a part of her feared that Nyxora was telling the truth.

Nyxora laughed, the sound sending chills down Sarah's spine. "Oh, little girl, I have no need to lie. You've seen it with your own eyes. The mark may fade, but the curse never left your family. It was passed down, generation to generation, until now. And Caitlin... sweet, fragile Caitlin... is the one who will bring it to fruition."

Sarah's mind raced, her heart pounding in her chest. She couldn't lose Caitlin. Not to this. Not to Nyxora.

"You won't have her," Sarah growled, her voice filled with fury. "I'll find a way to stop you. I'll break this curse. I won't let you take her."

Nyxora's eyes gleamed with amusement. "You're welcome to try," she sneered. "But the Blood Moon is rising, and with it, my power. You'll find that some things are beyond your control."

Without another word, Nyxora faded into the shadows, leaving behind only the suffocating darkness and the chilling echo of her voice.

Sarah turned her attention back to Caitlin, her heart pounding in her chest as she checked her sister's pulse again. It was still weak, her breathing shallow, but Caitlin was alive. She had a chance, but time was running out.

Nyxora's taunts echoed in Sarah's mind as she carefully laid Caitlin back down on the sofa. The curse was tied to their bloodline, to a deal made long ago. But how could she break something that had been passed down for generations?

Her mind raced back to the journals, the cryptic passages, the warnings about the Blood Moon and the veil between worlds. There had to be something, some clue she hadn't yet uncovered. Something she had missed.

With a renewed sense of urgency, Sarah rushed back to the stack of books and journals, flipping through the pages, searching for anything—any reference to the deal Nyxora had mentioned. Her eyes scanned the ancient texts, her breath coming in short, frantic gasps as the minutes ticked by.

And then she saw it.

A passage she had overlooked before, written in faded ink:

"When the Blood Moon rises, the veil between the worlds thins, and the curse draws near its fulfillment. But there is a way to sever the bond. A sacrifice—of blood and spirit—made willingly at the altar of the old gods, may break the curse and free the soul of the cursed one."

Sarah's heart skipped a beat. A sacrifice. Blood and spirit. That was the answer.

She glanced back at Caitlin, her sister's fragile form lying motionless on the sofa. A sacrifice? Sarah's mind raced, the implications of the passage settling over her like a heavy weight. If this was the only way to save Caitlin... could she do it? Could she risk her own life to break the curse?

There was no other choice.

Sarah stood up, determination flooding her veins. She knew what she had to do.

"I'll save you, Cait," she whispered, her voice steady despite the fear gnawing at her insides. "Even if it means giving everything."

With one last glance at Caitlin, Sarah grabbed the knife from the table and headed toward the door, the ancient passage ringing in her ears.

The altar of the old gods. The place where it all began.

She was going to end this.

For Caitlin.

For her family.

And for the generations to come.

Sarah's heart pounded in her chest, her mind racing to comprehend the enormity of what Nyxora had just revealed. The Blood Moon wasn't just a celestial event—it was a carefully orchestrated moment, tied to her family's suffering, designed to bridge two realms. And Caitlin, her sweet, fragile sister, was the key to unlocking it all.

She stared at Nyxora, her fists trembling at her sides, her voice shaking as she spoke. "You're lying. This can't be true. We were fighting to break the curse, not bring it to its end!"

Nyxora's smile only widened, her dark eyes gleaming with malicious delight. "Oh, Sarah, you poor, desperate fool. You've been playing right into my hands. Every fight, every sacrifice, every moment you thought you were defying fate... you were only helping to bring this moment closer."

Sarah's pulse quickened, her breaths coming in shallow gasps. "No," she whispered, her voice cracking. "This can't be happening. Caitlin can't be the key to... to something this dark. She's innocent. She didn't ask for this!"

Nyxora chuckled softly, her laughter cold and hollow. "Innocent? That doesn't matter. The curse is not concerned with innocence, Sarah. It never has been. Caitlin's fate was sealed the moment she was born into your family—into this cursed bloodline."

Sarah's eyes flicked to Caitlin, still unconscious on the sofa, her face pale, her breathing shallow. Tears welled in Sarah's eyes as the weight of Nyxora's words settled in her chest. Caitlin was the final piece in a puzzle that had been put into motion centuries before, long before either of them had been born.

But Sarah wasn't ready to give up. She wouldn't—she *couldn't*—let this be the end.

Her hands tightened into fists, and she looked back at Nyxora, fury burning in her chest. "I don't care what you say," she hissed, her voice trembling with emotion. "I won't let you use Caitlin for this. I'll stop you, even if it means giving everything I have."

Nyxora raised an eyebrow, a mocking smile playing at her lips. "And how do you plan to do that, little girl? You're nothing. You've always been nothing but an obstacle to me. The Blood Moon will rise, Caitlin will be mine, and there's nothing you can do to stop it."

Sarah's heart raced, fear clawing at her insides, but she refused to back down. She had faced Lethanor, faced death, and somehow survived. And now, with the stakes higher than ever, she would fight again—for Caitlin, for her family, for everything they had endured.

"You're wrong," Sarah whispered, her voice low but filled with determination. "I've always been more than you think."

With a final, venomous glance, Nyxora's figure began to fade into the shadows, her voice echoing through the room like a haunting melody. "We'll see, Sarah. The Blood Moon is coming. And when it does... we'll see just how much you're willing to sacrifice."

The room fell silent, the air thick with the lingering presence of darkness. Sarah's hands trembled as she knelt beside Caitlin, gently brushing a strand of hair from her sister's face. Her heart ached, her mind racing with fear and desperation, but deep down, she knew that Nyxora was right about one thing.

The Blood Moon was coming. And time was running out.

As Sarah sat beside Caitlin, her thoughts spun, searching for answers—anything that could help them. She needed a plan, a way to stop this before it was too late. The ancient texts had mentioned something about a sacrifice—blood and spirit—but the details had been cryptic, and Sarah didn't know what it truly meant.

But whatever it took, she was willing to do it. She would give everything to save Caitlin from this dark fate, even if it meant facing Nyxora head-on.

"I'll stop her," Sarah whispered, her voice filled with quiet determination. "I swear, Cait... I'll find a way to stop her."

And with that promise, Sarah stood, her heart pounding with the weight of the battle ahead. The Blood Moon was rising, but she would not let it be the end.

Not for Caitlin.

Not for her family.

And not for herself.

Caitlin stumbled off the sofa, her legs weak and trembling, as though they could barely hold her weight. Her vision blurred, the room tilting dangerously around her as she gripped the edge of the table for support. The voice in her head—Nyxora's dark, insidious whispers—continued to claw at her mind, filling her with dread and the suffocating belief that she was a danger to everyone around her. That she was a danger to Sarah.

"Caitlin, stop!" Sarah rushed forward, her arms outstretched, trying to steady her sister, but Caitlin jerked away, her heart pounding with fear.

"Don't touch me!" Caitlin cried, her voice breaking. She backed away, her eyes wide with panic. Tears streamed down her face as her body trembled violently. "I... I'm not safe. I'll hurt you, Sarah, I'll hurt you!"

Sarah froze, her heart breaking at the sight of her sister—once so full of life, now reduced to a terrified, trembling girl, fighting a battle against something they couldn't see or touch. Her voice softened, laced with desperation. "You won't hurt me, Cait. You never could. I'm here to protect you, and I'm not going anywhere."

But Caitlin shook her head frantically, her hands clawing at her temples as if trying to rip Nyxora's voice from her mind. "You don't understand!" she screamed. "Nyxora's inside me! She's... she's making me into something... something evil. I can't stop it!"

Sarah's breath caught in her throat. She had to find a way to calm Caitlin, to remind her of who she truly was beneath the curse. "You are not evil," Sarah said, stepping forward slowly, her hands raised in a gesture of peace. "You're my sister. The Caitlin I know would never give in to her. You're stronger than this."

But Caitlin's eyes were distant, glazed with fear and pain. Her body shook with the effort of holding back the darkness that threatened to consume her. Nyxora's voice slithered through her thoughts, louder now, taunting her. *She's wrong. You will hurt her. You'll destroy her, just like you destroyed them all.*

Caitlin let out a sob, falling to her knees, her hands still gripping her head as if trying to contain the pain. "I can't stop it, Sarah... I can't. Please, just... just go. You'll be safer if you leave me. I'm dangerous."

Sarah knelt beside her, gently placing her hands on Caitlin's shoulders, her voice trembling but resolute. "I'm not leaving you, Cait. Never. We're in this together, just like we've always been."

Caitlin's breath came in ragged gasps, her body tense with fear and uncertainty. "But Nyxora... she said—"

"I don't care what Nyxora said!" Sarah interrupted, her voice filled with raw emotion. "She's trying to break you, Cait, but she can't. You're stronger than her. You're stronger than this curse."

Caitlin stared at Sarah, her tear-streaked face filled with confusion and doubt. "I don't feel strong. I feel like I'm falling apart."

Sarah reached out, gently cupping Caitlin's face in her hands. "I know, Cait. I know this is hard, and I can't imagine how much pain you're in, but I believe in you. I *know* you can fight this. You've always been strong—even when you didn't feel it."

Caitlin's body trembled under the weight of Sarah's words, her heart torn between the love she felt for her sister and the fear that had consumed her for so long. The darkness inside her felt like a living thing, curling around her soul, threatening to pull her under. But Sarah's touch, her words—they were a lifeline, grounding Caitlin in a way that nothing else could.

For the first time in what felt like forever, Caitlin felt a flicker of hope. It was small, fragile, but it was there—fueled by Sarah's unwavering belief in her.

"I... I don't know if I can do this," Caitlin whispered, her voice barely audible.

Sarah smiled through her tears, brushing a strand of hair away from Caitlin's face. "You don't have to do it alone. I'm here, Cait. I'll always be here."

The room was silent for a long moment, save for the sound of their breathing. Caitlin, still trembling, slowly reached out and took Sarah's hand, gripping it tightly as if holding on for dear life.

Sarah squeezed her hand in return, her heart aching with love and fear for her sister. "We're going to get through this," she whispered, her voice filled with quiet determination. "We're going to face Nyxora together, and we're going to win. You hear me?"

Caitlin nodded slowly, her grip tightening on Sarah's hand. The fear was still there, lurking at the edges of her mind, but for the first time, it didn't feel overwhelming. With Sarah by her side, she felt like she had a chance—a chance to fight back against the darkness that had been clawing at her soul for so long.

And as the shadow of the Blood Moon loomed ever closer, Caitlin knew that whatever happened next, she wouldn't face it alone.

Sarah's entire body shook with fury, fear, and desperation. She knelt beside Caitlin, trying to hold her sister steady, to stop the violent convulsions wracking her frail form. The air around them pulsed with the eerie, suffocating red glow from the Blood Moon, but Sarah's focus was entirely on Caitlin—her little sister, the one she had sworn to protect at all costs.

"You're wrong, Nyxora," Sarah spat through gritted teeth, refusing to let the dark creature's words take hold in her mind. "Caitlin isn't gone. She's still in there, and I'm going to bring her back."

Nyxora stood still, watching Sarah's efforts with a cold amusement. "You truly think you can defy fate? You're not just fighting me, Sarah. You're fighting the very forces that have bound your family for centuries. And you're fighting Caitlin's own destiny. It was written in the stars long before you were born. This is her fate."

Sarah's heart ached as she looked at Caitlin's pale, trembling body, her face contorted in pain. The red light in her eyes flickered again, as if some terrible power was trying to claw its way out. But Sarah knew her sister was still in there—somewhere, beneath the pain and darkness, Caitlin was fighting too.

"No," Sarah said, her voice cracking but resolute. "I don't care what fate says. I don't care about this curse or the Blood Moon. I'm not losing her, Nyxora. Not to you."

Nyxora's eyes gleamed with sinister amusement, and her voice dropped to a menacing whisper. "You don't have the strength to save her, Sarah. Your love, your bond... it's all meaningless in the face of what's coming. The Blood Moon is awakening her true nature, and soon, she'll be lost to the darkness forever."

But Sarah wasn't listening. She couldn't listen. She couldn't afford to let Nyxora's poison seep into her thoughts. Her focus remained entirely on Caitlin—on the little girl who had always believed in her big sister's strength, even when Sarah had doubted it herself. And now, in this moment, Sarah refused to give up.

With trembling hands, Sarah reached out and cupped Caitlin's face, her fingers gently brushing away the sweat-soaked strands of hair sticking to her sister's forehead. "Cait... I know you're scared. I know it feels like the darkness is winning, but you're stronger than this. You can fight it, I know you can."

Caitlin's body convulsed again, her breath coming in short, ragged gasps, but Sarah didn't let go. She held on tighter, her voice soft but firm. "You're not alone, Cait. I'm right here. You've always been strong enough to fight this. Don't let her win."

For a brief, agonizing moment, it seemed like Caitlin couldn't hear her—like the darkness was too deep, too suffocating. But then, slowly, Caitlin's eyes flickered again, the crimson glow dimming just enough for Sarah to see a flash of recognition, a spark of the girl she knew.

"Sarah..." Caitlin's voice was barely a whisper, her body trembling with exhaustion and pain. Tears welled up in her eyes as she looked at her sister, her voice fragile. "I... I don't want to hurt you. I don't want to be this."

"You won't," Sarah promised, her heart pounding. "You're not a monster, Cait. You never were. We're going to fight this together, okay? Just hold on. Stay with me."

Nyxora's laughter cut through the room like ice, cold and mocking. "You're delaying the inevitable, Sarah. The Blood Moon is rising, and with every second, Caitlin is slipping further away. There's nothing you can do."

But Sarah refused to give in. She pressed her forehead against Caitlin's, her voice barely above a whisper but filled with fierce determination. "I love you, Cait. You're stronger than this curse. Stronger than Nyxora. You just have to fight a little longer."

Caitlin's breath hitched, her body still trembling, but Sarah could feel it—the faintest stirrings of hope, of fight, returning to her sister. It wasn't over yet.

"Come on, Cait," Sarah urged, her voice thick with emotion. "We're going to beat this. You and me, like always."

For the first time in what felt like forever, Caitlin's body stilled, the violent convulsions subsiding as she focused on Sarah's voice. The red glow in her eyes faded slightly, and for just a moment, the Caitlin that Sarah knew—the girl who had always looked up to her with love and trust—was there again.

Nyxora's cruel smile faltered, her eyes narrowing as she watched the scene unfold. "This won't last," she hissed, her voice filled with venom. "The Blood Moon's power is too strong. She will break."

But Sarah ignored her, her focus entirely on Caitlin. "We're going to make it through this," she whispered. "I won't let go, Cait. I won't lose you."

And as the Blood Moon loomed overhead, its crimson light casting an eerie glow over the room, Sarah held onto Caitlin, refusing to let the darkness win. They had faced impossible odds before, and now, in this moment of unimaginable fear and pain, Sarah knew one thing for certain: she would fight for her sister, no matter what it took.

They weren't done yet.

Sarah's heart leaped at the sound of Caitlin's voice, weak but unmistakable. Her breath hitched, and she spun around, eyes wide with hope. Caitlin's once rigid body trembled slightly, her lips barely moving as she tried to speak. The glow in her eyes had dimmed, just a fraction, but enough to give Sarah hope that her sister was still in there, fighting.

"Cait!" Sarah rushed to her side, falling to her knees in front of her. She gently cupped Caitlin's face, her hands trembling. "I'm here, Cait. I'm right here. You're not gone. I know you can hear me."

Caitlin's red-tinged eyes flickered as if struggling to focus. Her body remained stiff, but her lips parted again, another whisper escaping. "I... don't... want this."

Sarah's chest tightened with emotion, tears welling up in her eyes. "You don't have to give in, Cait. I know you're stronger than this. Fight it, please. You're not alone."

Nyxora's mocking laughter filled the room, cutting through the fragile moment like a knife. "How touching," she sneered, her voice dripping with cruelty. "But it's pointless, Sarah. She's already mine, and no amount of pleading will change that."

Sarah's fury reignited, burning hot in her chest. She stood abruptly, turning to face Nyxora with fire in her eyes. "You don't get to decide that!" she shouted, her voice shaking with determination. "You may have cursed our family, but you will not take Caitlin. I will not let you."

Nyxora's expression hardened, her amusement fading into cold anger. "You're a fool, Sarah. This isn't about you. The Blood Moon has risen, and Caitlin's fate is sealed. You cannot stop what's coming."

Sarah's hands clenched into fists at her sides. "Watch me," she snarled. "You've underestimated me before, Nyxora. And you're making the same mistake again."

Nyxora's eyes darkened, her lips curling into a malicious smile. "And what exactly do you think you can do? The curse has been written in blood. It's as old as time itself. Do you really think you can break it with love? With your feeble attempts to protect her?"

Sarah didn't flinch, her voice steady and filled with conviction. "I don't know how to break the curse. But I do know one thing—I'm not letting Caitlin go without a fight. You think you've won, but you don't know us. You don't know what we're capable of when we're together."

She turned back to Caitlin, her heart breaking at the sight of her sister's pale face, her body still caught in the grip of Nyxora's curse. But she refused to give in to despair. Caitlin had fought too hard, survived too much for it to end like this. There had to be a way. There had to be something she could do.

"Cait, I know you're scared," Sarah whispered, kneeling beside her again. "But you've got to fight. I'm with you, every step of the way. We're stronger together. We always have been."

Caitlin's body trembled, her breath ragged and shallow. But then, ever so faintly, her hand moved—just enough for Sarah to feel it.

Nyxora's eyes narrowed, her face twisting with frustration. "Enough of this," she hissed, stepping forward, her presence filling the room with dark energy. "You cannot defy the Blood Moon. The curse will be completed. Caitlin's blood will spill, and the doorway between realms will open."

But before Nyxora could make another move, Sarah stood tall, blocking her path. "You're wrong, Nyxora," she said, her voice firm. "Caitlin's blood may be the key, but you forgot one thing."

Nyxora raised an eyebrow, her expression filled with cruel amusement. "And what's that?"

Sarah's eyes burned with determination as she stared Nyxora down. "You forgot that I'm her sister. And I will protect her with everything I have."

Without warning, Sarah reached out and grabbed Caitlin's hand, holding it tightly. In that moment, she could feel the connection between them—the bond that had always been there, stronger than any curse or darkness that tried to tear them apart.

Nyxora's eyes widened in realization, her voice laced with fury. "What are you doing?!" she spat, stepping back as the air around them began to shift.

But Sarah didn't waver. "We've faced everything together, Cait. And this will be no different. You're not doing this alone."

A surge of warmth spread through Sarah's body, her connection to Caitlin growing stronger. The room seemed to vibrate with energy, and for the first time, the red glow from the Blood Moon began to waver, flickering as if something was pushing back against it.

Caitlin's eyes fluttered open, the red light in them dimming even further. Her voice, weak but filled with emotion, whispered, "Sarah?"

"I'm right here, Cait," Sarah whispered back, tears spilling down her cheeks. "I'm not leaving you."

Nyxora's voice trembled with rage, her dark form flickering as the bond between the sisters grew stronger. "You... cannot... win!" she hissed, her words filled with venom.

But Sarah only held onto Caitlin tighter, her voice steady and full of love. "We already have."

Sarah's heart pounded in her chest as she cradled Caitlin, her breath ragged with fear. The cold, unnatural silence in the room pressed down on her like a suffocating weight. She stared down at her sister's pale face, her own tears falling unchecked. Caitlin's breaths were so faint, so shallow, it was as if life itself was slipping away with every second.

"No... Cait," Sarah whispered, her voice trembling. She tightened her hold on Caitlin, her hands shaking as she brushed a stray lock of hair from her sister's face. "I'm not losing you... not like this."

But deep down, the despair gnawed at her. Nyxora's cruel words echoed in her mind, the chilling promise that Caitlin's fate was sealed. Sarah clenched her fists, her nails digging into her palms, refusing to give in to the hopelessness threatening to consume her.

"Please, Caitlin... fight," Sarah whispered desperately, her voice raw. "I know you're still in there."

But Caitlin remained still, her body lifeless in Sarah's arms. The red glow of the Blood Moon continued to bathe the room in its eerie light, a constant reminder of the curse's presence, looming over them like a specter.

Suddenly, a faint flicker of movement caught Sarah's eye. Caitlin's fingers twitched, just barely, but it was enough for Sarah to notice.

"Cait?" Sarah breathed, hope surging within her. She leaned closer, her heart racing as she watched her sister closely. "Come on, Caitlin... I know you can hear me."

For a moment, it seemed like nothing would change. But then Caitlin's eyes fluttered open, the faintest glimmer of recognition in them. The red glow had dimmed slightly, and Sarah could see a trace of her sister's true self breaking through.

"Sarah..." Caitlin's voice was barely a whisper, weak and filled with pain, but it was there. Her lips trembled, and her hand reached out, grasping at the air as if searching for something solid to hold onto.

Sarah quickly took Caitlin's hand, squeezing it tightly. "I'm right here, Cait. I'm not leaving you."

Caitlin's eyes filled with tears, her body trembling in Sarah's arms. "I... I'm scared," she choked out, her voice fragile. "She's in my head... I don't know if I can fight her."

"You're not alone," Sarah said fiercely, holding onto her sister's hand like a lifeline. "We're in this together, Cait. We've always been stronger together."

Caitlin's grip tightened, and for the first time, the red in her eyes flickered again, dimming further. The curse was still there, the Blood Moon's power still looming, but for now, Caitlin was fighting it. And that was enough for Sarah.

"I'm here," Sarah whispered, pressing her forehead against Caitlin's. "We'll fight her. We'll fight this curse. I'm not letting you go."

Suddenly, Caitlin's body tensed, her eyes snapping open in terror. Her breathing quickened, and her hand tightened around Sarah's. "It's happening," she gasped, her voice shaking with fear. "Sarah... I don't want to... I don't want to become her."

Sarah's heart shattered at the fear in Caitlin's voice. She knelt beside her sister, her hand gently stroking Caitlin's hair, trying to calm her despite the panic surging through her own body. "You're not going to become her," Sarah said firmly, though her voice trembled with the weight of her own doubt. "We're going to stop this."

But Caitlin's eyes were wide with terror, her body trembling as the curse's power surged through her. "I don't... I don't know if I can fight it anymore," she whispered, her voice barely audible.

The red light of the Blood Moon intensified, casting everything in a sickening glow. Sarah could feel the weight of it pressing down on them, the curse creeping closer with every passing second.

"No," Sarah whispered fiercely, her voice breaking. She took Caitlin's hand in both of hers, her grip tight and desperate. "You're stronger than this, Cait. You can fight her. You have to."

Caitlin's breathing grew more ragged, her eyes fluttering as the dark energy within her surged. But then, for a brief moment, her gaze locked with Sarah's, and a flicker of determination passed between them.

"I'll... try," Caitlin whispered, her voice trembling with fear and exhaustion.

Sarah nodded, her heart pounding in her chest as she held onto that glimmer of hope. "I'm right here with you," she whispered. "We'll fight her together."

And as the Blood Moon's light pulsed around them, Sarah held onto her sister, refusing to let go. She would fight for Caitlin with everything she had, no matter what it took.

Because she wasn't just fighting for Caitlin's life.

She was fighting for Caitlin's soul.

Sarah screamed, her voice breaking as she fought against the invisible force pinning her down. "No! Caitlin! Stop it!" Her cries were desperate, filled with a raw, primal terror as she watched Nyxora's blade cut into Caitlin's arm, spilling her blood onto the ancient stone.

The crimson liquid dripped slowly, pooling on the altar and shimmering in the light of the Blood Moon. The air pulsed with dark energy, and the ground beneath them trembled as if the earth itself was responding to the ancient ritual being fulfilled. Caitlin's body remained limp, her eyes open but unseeing, as if the life had already been drained from her.

Nyxora's laughter echoed through the clearing, cold and triumphant. "It's too late, Sarah," she taunted, her voice filled with cruel satisfaction. "The Blood Moon has accepted her blood. The gate between realms is opening. Soon, everything you love will be gone."

A low, ominous rumble shook the ground as the shadows around the altar swirled faster, growing more chaotic with each passing second.

Sarah, still struggling against the invisible force, felt the weight of hopelessness crushing her chest. She couldn't get to Caitlin. She couldn't stop this.

But as the darkness around Caitlin deepened, something flickered—something small, but unmistakable. Caitlin's hand twitched, just barely, but enough for Sarah to notice. Hope surged in Sarah's chest, a desperate, fragile hope, but it was enough to give her strength.

"Caitlin!" Sarah screamed, her voice filled with urgency. "Fight it! Please, you have to fight!"

For a moment, there was nothing—just the relentless pull of the dark magic surrounding the altar. But then, Caitlin's eyes fluttered, the faintest flicker of life returning to them. Her lips parted, and a weak, ragged breath escaped her.

Nyxora's smile faltered, her eyes narrowing as she noticed the change in Caitlin. "What—" she began, but before she could finish, Caitlin's body jerked, her hand moving slightly as if trying to lift itself.

"Caitlin, you can do this!" Sarah cried, tears streaming down her face. "Don't let her win! I'm right here!"

Caitlin's breathing grew more labored, but the flicker of life in her eyes strengthened. Her hand moved again, this time more deliberately, her fingers curling slightly as if grasping for something—anything to hold onto.

"No!" Nyxora snarled, her voice filled with fury. She raised the blade again, intending to strike Caitlin once more, but before she could bring it down, a burst of energy erupted from the altar, throwing her back. Nyxora staggered, her expression twisting with rage and disbelief as she watched Caitlin's body begin to glow faintly, a soft, golden light pushing back against the shadows.

Sarah's breath caught in her throat. She could feel it—the power surging within Caitlin, a force that wasn't just dark or corrupted. It was something deeper, something pure. It was Caitlin's strength, her will to fight, to resist the curse that had been placed upon her.

Nyxora hissed, her eyes blazing with anger as she stepped forward again. "You think you can stop this?" she spat, her voice venomous. "You are nothing, Caitlin! Your fate was sealed the moment you were born!"

But Caitlin's body continued to glow, the golden light growing stronger, pushing back the crimson haze of the Blood Moon. Her hand twitched again, and this time, her fingers closed around Sarah's. The touch was weak, but it was there.

Sarah sobbed, her heart pounding in her chest. "Cait... I'm here," she whispered, squeezing Caitlin's hand as tightly as she could. "I'm not letting go."

The energy around Caitlin pulsed, and for the first time, Sarah could feel the darkness beginning to waver. The shadows that had coiled around the altar flickered, as if unsure of themselves, and the ground beneath them seemed to still.

Nyxora's fury only grew, her face contorting with rage. "No! This isn't possible!" she shrieked, her voice cracking as she reached for Caitlin, her hand outstretched. "You belong to me!"

But before she could touch Caitlin, the golden light around her exploded outward, sending Nyxora flying back once again. The shadows recoiled, retreating from Caitlin's body as the golden glow enveloped her completely.

Sarah gasped, her hand still gripping Caitlin's as the light filled the clearing, casting away the darkness. She could feel Caitlin's pulse now—weak, but steady. Her sister was fighting. She was still there.

Nyxora, now lying on the ground, snarled in frustration, her eyes blazing with hatred. "This changes nothing!" she screamed. "The curse cannot be broken!"

But Sarah, her heart filled with renewed strength, stood tall. She looked down at her sister, her voice steady and full of love. "We're breaking it," she said softly, her words meant for Caitlin. "You and me, together."

The crimson light of the Blood Moon began to fade, its ominous glow dimming as Caitlin's golden light grew brighter. The curse that had bound her, that had threatened to consume her, was unraveling. Slowly, the shadows receded, and the oppressive weight of the dark magic lifted.

Nyxora's screams filled the air, but they were drowned out by the power radiating from Caitlin's body. The connection between the Blood Moon and the ancient curse was severing, the dark magic fraying and collapsing in on itself.

Sarah held onto Caitlin's hand, tears of relief streaming down her face. "You did it, Cait," she whispered, her voice filled with awe. "You're still here."

And as the last of the shadows dissolved into nothingness, Caitlin's eyes fluttered open, her gaze locking with Sarah's. She smiled, weak but filled with love.

"I told you," Caitlin whispered, her voice barely audible but full of warmth. "I'm not going anywhere."

Sarah laughed through her tears, leaning down to press her forehead against Caitlin's. "I never doubted you for a second."

Together, they had broken the curse.

As Nyxora hurled her magic toward Caitlin, the dark bolt crackled through the air like a viper, aimed directly at the heart of the power that now consumed Sarah's sister. But before it could strike, something extraordinary happened. Caitlin's eyes—those glowing, blood-red eyes—flared with a brilliance that seemed to defy the very darkness engulfing her.

The bolt of magic collided with the energy swirling around Caitlin but didn't penetrate. Instead, it rebounded, backfiring toward Nyxora with a blinding flash of light. Nyxora's face twisted in horror as the force of her own magic slammed into her chest, sending her flying back into the twisted trees with a scream of pure rage. The impact was violent, the sound of cracking bones echoing through the clearing.

Sarah, gasping for breath, forced herself to her feet. Her body trembled, battered by the force of the magic around her, but she refused to let go of the hope flickering inside her. The sight of Caitlin, still suspended in the air, tore at her heart. Her sister's face was a mask of pain, her body convulsing under the pressure of the power surging through her.

"Caitlin!" Sarah screamed, her voice raw with desperation. She stumbled forward, arms outstretched, willing herself to get closer, to reach Caitlin before it was too late. "You have to fight it! You can't let her win!"

But Caitlin's eyes—those eyes that once held warmth, humor, and love—were nearly consumed by the glow of the Blood Moon's light. Her body trembled as the last remnants of her own spirit seemed to battle with the curse trying to claim her.

"Sarah..." Caitlin's voice came out as a broken whisper, barely audible, but it was enough to make Sarah stop in her tracks. The flicker of recognition—the tiny glimmer of her sister still inside—gave Sarah the strength to keep going.

"You're still in there, Cait," Sarah whispered, tears streaming down her face. "I know you are."

The ground trembled violently beneath them, the air vibrating with dark energy as the ritual continued to spiral out of control. But Sarah refused to let go, refused to believe this was how it ended.

She reached the base of the stone altar, her hands trembling as she grabbed onto the edge. She pulled herself up, her knees bruised from the jagged stone, and climbed to where Caitlin hovered, inches above the ancient surface. Her sister's body was limp, her chest rising and falling with shallow breaths, but the power radiating from her was palpable. It was as if the magic of the Blood Moon had fused with her very being.

"I won't let you go," Sarah whispered fiercely, her voice shaking as she reached out to touch Caitlin's hand. "Not like this."

The moment her fingers made contact with Caitlin's, a shockwave of energy rippled through her body. Sarah gasped as the force of the magic surged through her veins, nearly knocking her back, but she held on. She wasn't going to let go—not now, not ever.

Caitlin's eyes, still glowing with the light of the Blood Moon, flickered once again. Her lips parted, and Sarah could hear her sister's voice, so faint, so fragile, as if she were trying to break free.

"I... I can't hold on..." Caitlin's voice wavered, her breath coming in ragged gasps. "It's too strong, Sarah. I... I'm slipping."

Sarah's heart shattered at the sound of Caitlin's words, but she refused to give in to the fear clawing at her insides. "You're not slipping, Cait," she said, her voice filled with fierce determination. "You're still here, and I'm not letting go."

She could feel it now—the connection between them, the bond that had always tied them together, stronger than any curse or magic. Sarah focused on that, on the love she had for her sister, the memories they shared, the promise she had made to always protect her.

"You can fight this," Sarah whispered, her grip tightening on Caitlin's hand. "I know you can."

The magic around them swirled violently, the shadows deepening, but as Sarah's words reached Caitlin, something shifted. The red glow in Caitlin's eyes dimmed, just for a moment, as if the power of the Blood Moon was losing its grip.

"No!" Nyxora's voice echoed from the shadows, filled with fury. She stumbled back toward the clearing, her body battered, but her eyes blazing with hatred. "You can't break the curse! She belongs to me!"

But Sarah ignored her. All her focus, all her energy, was on Caitlin. "Caitlin," she whispered again, her voice soft but unwavering. "Come back to me."

For a moment, everything seemed to pause—the swirling magic, the trembling earth, even the hum of the Blood Moon's power. Caitlin's eyes fluttered, and for the first time since the ritual had begun, Sarah saw her sister's gaze—clear, untainted by the darkness that had consumed her.

"Sarah..." Caitlin's voice was barely a whisper, but it was her. It was Caitlin.

Sarah's heart leapt in her chest, and she squeezed Caitlin's hand tighter, her tears falling freely. "I'm right here, Cait," she whispered, her voice trembling with emotion. "You're not alone."

The red glow in Caitlin's eyes faded further, the dark magic around her beginning to weaken. But the Blood Moon's power still clung to her, refusing to let go completely.

Nyxora, her face twisted with rage, raised her hands, summoning the last of her strength. "No! I will not lose to you!" she screamed, her voice filled with venom as she unleashed a final surge of dark magic toward the altar.

But before the magic could reach Caitlin, a brilliant light erupted from her body, pushing back the darkness. The light—pure, golden, and filled with warmth—surged outward, breaking through the hold of the Blood Moon.

Nyxora's magic disintegrated on contact, her scream of fury drowned out by the light. The dark tendrils of magic around Caitlin shattered, and the Blood Moon's crimson glow dimmed, retreating into the sky.

Caitlin's body collapsed onto the altar, her breath shallow, but she was free. The curse was broken.

Sarah sobbed with relief, pulling her sister into her arms. "You did it," she whispered, her voice filled with awe. "You're safe."

Caitlin, weak but alive, rested her head against Sarah's shoulder, her voice barely audible as she whispered, "We did it... together."

And as the Blood Moon faded from the sky, the darkness that had haunted them for so long finally lifted, leaving only the bond between two sisters—unbroken, and stronger than ever.

As Caitlin and Sarah walked together, the weight of everything that had happened slowly began to settle into the background. The sun rose higher, casting long shadows behind them, but the warmth of the morning light seemed to promise a new beginning—a future that was no longer dictated by the darkness of the Blood Moon.

Caitlin, still adjusting to the immense power she now held, felt a strange calm wash over her. It wasn't the same as before. She wasn't the same. But she was still herself—still Caitlin, still the sister Sarah had fought so hard to save. And though the shadows of Nyxora's magic lingered in her blood, she knew, deep down, she had won. They had won.

As they reached the edge of the forest, the clearing behind them disappearing from view, Sarah glanced over at Caitlin, her smile full of relief and a touch of wonder. "So... what now?" she asked, her tone light but edged with the reality of all they still had to figure out.

Caitlin raised an eyebrow, her lips quirking into a smirk. "I guess I could start by not accidentally summoning dark magic during breakfast."

Sarah laughed softly, the sound carrying on the morning breeze. "Yeah, I think we've had enough magical disasters to last a lifetime."

They walked in silence for a while, the road ahead stretching into the unknown, but it no longer felt daunting. Instead, it felt like the start of something new—an adventure that, while uncertain, was theirs to navigate together.

Caitlin tilted her head, the sun warming her skin. "Hey, Sarah?"

"Yeah?"

"Thanks for being my hero."

Sarah's heart swelled at the words, and she gave Caitlin a teasing nudge. "You know, it's exhausting saving your butt all the time."

Caitlin grinned, the teasing glint in her eyes undeniable. "You love it."

Sarah sighed dramatically. "Yeah, yeah. What would you do without me?"

Caitlin shrugged, her smile softening. "I guess we'll never have to find out."

Sarah's heart swelled at the words, and she gave Caitlin a teasing nudge. "You know, it's exhausting saving your butt all the time."

Caitlin grinned, the teasing glint in her eyes undeniable. "You love it."

Sarah sighed dramatically. "Yeah, yeah. What would you do without me?"

Caitlin shrugged, her smile softening. "I guess we'll never have to find out."

And with that, the two sisters continued on, walking toward a horizon no longer filled with curses or Blood Moons, but with hope, laughter, and the unbreakable bond they would always share.